HOW THE B*TCH STOLE CHRISTMAS

Evergreen Valley Holidays

SHANNON O'CONNOR

Cover Art by *Rieley Stephens.*

Typography by *M Leigh Morhaime of Lost Marbles Design.*

Edited & Proofread by Victoria Ellis of *Cruel Ink Editing & Design.*

Formatted by Shannon O'Connor.

❀ Formatted with Vellum

Content Warnings

Fat-phobia
- on page description

Please also note I am not a lawyer nor real estate agent, this book is a work of fiction and I have had to do a little "bending" with the laws to make this story come together. Just like a Hallmark movie we don't question how no one seems to have a "real" job, it's holiday magic that brings this story together.

To my Grandma.

El
_____

"El, your phone has been ringing off the hook," my assistant tells me as I return from my weekly client meeting.

"Who is it?" I ask, but as if on cue, the phone starts ringing again, and she drops to her chair to answer it.

"Eliora Monroe's office." There's a pause. "Yes, sir. Please hold." She puts the call on hold and looks at me. "It's your father, and he says it's urgent."

"I'll take it in my office." I sigh. My father doesn't usually call me at work, so it must be something important.

I close my office door behind me and take a seat at my oversized desk, taking a deep breath before I answer the call just as I would before any temperamental client.

"Hello?" I answer.

"It's about time. Why does it take so much effort for your father to get through?" My father huffs on the other end.

"I was in a meeting, and my assistant knows not to interrupt me for any reason," I explain.

"Well, I need you to come home."

"To my apartment?" I ask, confused. Surely, he didn't mean

back to the town I grew up in? I haven't been back there in years, and it's better that way.

"No, back to Evergreen Valley. I need your help closing this deal. There has to be a way around this contract, and I don't know real estate law like you do." It must be important if my father is admitting he doesn't know how something works.

"I-I can't just leave work. I have clients and a busy schedule. I'm weeks away from becoming a partner," I say.

"Eliora, I promised you when you moved away that I wouldn't ask you to come home. But this is important to me, to the family, and I'm asking." He sighs. I hate that my father actually sounds desperate. This isn't his usual tone at all.

"What's the contract? Maybe I can look it over here and send you my thoughts without coming over," I suggest.

The silence on the other end is so long that I almost think he's hung up on me. It honestly wouldn't be the first time. But I look at the call and see he's still on the line.

He sighs before speaking. "Your grandfather is almost eighty, and as much as we'd all like to pretend that his health isn't declining, he's not going to be around forever. It's important to him that we finish this contract before he's gone."

Now I'm the one sighing. He's guilt tripping me with my grandfather. He's close to eighty, and we all know about his ongoing battle to take over the town's local bookstore. I don't know all the details, but I know he's made it his life's work to take it over. He's acquired most of the other properties in Evergreen Valley, and he even built an area of high-rise apartments. At some point, he'll have control over a majority of the town. But the thing that's most important is that tiny little bookstore on the edge of town. I don't know if it's about the property itself, or the building, or what, but I know how important it is to the family.

"Fine, but I'm only coming home for a weekend," I say. "I'll look it over, offer my advice and whatever help I can, but that's all I can do."

"Okay, thank you Eliora. I appreciate this."

"I'll look over my schedule with my assistant and let you know the earliest I can visit," I tell him.

"Okay."

We hang up without any pleasantries. I'm pretty sure that's the longest conversation I've had with him in years. My father and I aren't particularly close. It isn't that we fight or have any animosity toward each other, but he's a tough person to be close to. He's a businessman, and that's always been his number one priority in life. My mother hasn't ever been much better, always wanting the finer things in life and not bothering to pay much attention to me or my little sister. That's why, the second I could, I applied to colleges in the city and moved here right after high school graduation. Of course, their financial support didn't hurt. I definitely couldn't have made it this far without their help.

"El, you're free the first weekend of December to visit your father. Should I mark that down?" my assistant, Leah, asks, peeking her head into my office.

"Yes please, and bring me the Bartz contract, please. I need to look it over before our dinner tonight," I instruct.

"Got it," she says with a smile.

Once Leah brings me the contract, I'm back in work mode. I try to push my father and anything else going on in my life out of my head. I like to focus on work at work, and anything personal on my own time. That's how I'm going to make partner before I turn thirty. The meeting tonight was pretty straightfor-ward. The client is inheriting their family's ranch in North Carolina and wants to sell it without having to actually go there. It won't be a hard sell. The place is gorgeous, and it's accessible to town. He needs to sign some papers for me, and then I can put out official feelers for the property—but I have no doubt the ranch will sell by the end of the year.

My personal phone rings, and I smile when I see my best friend Bells's name and drunk profile photo appear on my screen.

"Well look who took the time to finally call me back," I tease.

We've been texting all day, but she hasn't called me back in a few days.

"Hey, you know I'm in the process of closing things up for the winter," she explains. Bells recently inherited an apple orchard, and despite being as much of a city girl as I am, she surprised everyone by taking it over. I think it also has to do with the hot farmhand she fell in love with.

"Any idea when you're coming back to pack up your stuff?" I ask. She's been subletting her apartment while she decided if she was serious about the small-town life or not. But now she's making the move permanently and wants to pack up the rest of her things.

"That's why I'm calling. I have movers coming tomorrow for the rest of my things, and I want to be there so they don't drop or forget anything, but could we grab drinks tonight?" Bells asks.

"I have a client meeting at five that should be done by six. Can we grab drinks at seven?" I ask, looking over my calendar.

"Yes please. The usual place?"

"I'll text Sawyer and see if I can get our usual table at Puzzles," I add with a smile.

"Yes! I've been dying for her mixed drinks. They don't make the same things up here. I keep trying to convince the bartender to take a mixology class, but he thinks I'm joking. I'm stuck with the same three mixed drinks, and it's sort of boring." She sighs.

"That's what you get for moving up to a small town and leaving your best friend behind," I tease.

"Come on, it's not like you're alone. You have Tara," she points out, and I feel the realization hit me like a ton of bricks. I forgot about the woman I've been living with and dating for the past few years.

"You're right." I try to laugh off, but I know it's no use with Bells.

"What's going on? Did something happen?" she asks, picking up on my tone.

"Can we talk about it later? I don't wanna get into it at work," I say quietly.

"Of course. I'll see you later. Bye!"

"Bye!" My relationship with Tara is complicated. I don't want to get into it while I'm at work. It's better to have that conversation over drinks.

I collect my things and head downstairs for the afternoon staff meeting. Leah brings her notepad and grabs me a latte on the way. She takes more notes than I do at the staff meetings, but it's important that I show up. I glance at my texts before I turn the ringer off and notice there aren't any texts from Tara. I didn't think there would be, so I'm not sure why I wanted to hurt my own feelings by checking.

By the time the meeting is over, I head toward my downtown office for my meeting with Bartz. It only takes a half an hour to explain everything in the contract, have them sign it, and head home to change. Thankfully, Tara isn't home, so I don't have to get into it with her on my way out the door. After changing into something more appropriate for after work, I head across town to meet Bells for drinks at our favorite bar.

"ELLLLL!" Bells screams when she sees me. I race over, and we hug tightly. It's been too long since I've seen her in person. Her auburn curls cascade around her face as she grins at me.

"Did you get shorter?" I ask, and then I gasp when I see her wearing shoes without a heel.

"Oh shush. I forgot to pack my heels, so I'm stuck with these boots. But they're designer so they're still cute." She laughs. I give myself a second to take her in. She looks calmer. She has on her bright red lipstick—her signature look—but her smile seems more relaxed. Her clothes are still name-brand, but they're more small-town chic than city chic.

"How are you? Tell me everything about Tilly and the place," I say as I wave over the waiter to grab us some drinks.

"It's great! Tilly and I are still using our own houses, but we take turns spending the night at each other's places. We don't want to rush anything by moving in together too fast. The orchard did really well this fall, so we can afford to shut down completely for the winter. We're keeping the bakery open because Lina loves it, but we don't have to," she says proudly. When she first got there, the place was almost bankrupt. The waiter comes over, and we each order a cocktail.

"I'm so glad it worked out for you. It must be serious if you're moving your stuff out of the city."

"It is. I never thought I'd say it, but I really love the small town. Sapphire Falls is just so different than anywhere else," she gushes.

"Promise you'll at least come and visit sometimes," I say.

"Of course. And you're always welcome to come visit and stay with us, too. But I know all about your aversion to small towns," Bells says.

"Yeah, about that… My father actually called today and insisted I visit home. I have to help them with a contract at the beginning of December." I sigh.

"Wow, it must be important if they're asking you and you're actually going." She sips her drink.

"He sort of guilted me into it. But I made him promise it was one weekend and that's all," I explain.

"Well, at least that's good. Is Tara going with you?" Bells asks, and I know it's her sly way of trying to find out what's going on with us.

"I have no idea. I didn't even talk to her about it yet, so probably not." I shrug.

"And you're being all coy about her because…?"

"We're sort of fighting again." I hate admitting that out loud. Tara and I have been together for almost five years, and we've spent the majority of them fighting with each other.

"What happened this time?" She sighs.

"I don't know. Nothing really *happened*, but she's upset that she's not going home for Christmas. I told her she can go, but her family is taking a vacation to the Bahamas for once. They even invited me, but I said no," I explain.

"Are you still on bad terms with her family?" Bells asks. She remembers the last time I saw them—they all but fat-shamed me, and Tara did nothing to stop it.

"I just don't talk to them. She knows how I feel about it, so I'm surprised she'd even ask. I think she'd have fun without me, but she doesn't want me being alone for Christmas—which is stupid, because I'll probably be working anyway." I frown.

"I gotta ask, and I know you hate when I do, but I'm your best friend so I have to. Do you still love Tara? Because it seems like you're with her more out of obligation or complacency than love at this point." Bells looks at me intently.

I don't bother lying to her. She's my best friend, and I know there's no judgment here. But I don't know the answer. We've been together for so many years, so at this point, it seems silly to throw in the towel. But is that a good enough reason to stay together? For the most part, we don't even talk anymore. I get home long after she's already in bed, and we haven't had sex in months. There's no intimacy—or even talking—between us anymore. I sleep on the couch most of the time, because it's easier than facing her if she is still awake. We're more like room-mates than a couple at this point. I hate it, but I also can't bring myself to end it. She has good qualities—*great* qualities, even— so what if we don't have that spark anymore? Doesn't that just mean we've grown into something else?

"I love her, but I don't know. I feel like when you've been with someone for a while things just become calmer. It's just easier that way sometimes," I say.

"I'm never going to tell you what to do and how to live your life, but maybe you should think more about if that's what you want for the rest of your life. Because you don't seem happy with her like you were in the beginning," she says, and I can tell she's treading carefully.

"Is anyone ever as happy once the honeymoon period wears off?" I ask.

"Maybe. I've seen couples who have been together twenty years and still look as happy as Tilly and I are. I think it's about knowing what you want and not settling for anything that doesn't feel *exactly* right," Bells says.

"I am so going to miss you psychoanalyzing my relationship now that you're leaving me for the country," I tease with the hint of a fake country accent.

"Oh please, you could never get rid of me. I'll be less than two hours away, and I can still tell it like it is whenever you want me to. But I can tell you wanna change the subject, so tell me about work instead." She smiles, and I'm relieved we can move on from my relationship woes.

TWO

Jax
___

"**C**an I help you with anything?" I ask before looking up from the book I'm putting on the shelf. The bells above the front door jingle to let me know someone's walking in.

"I've been telling you for years to let me take this place off your hands." The voice sends shivers down my spine, and I know it all too well. Mr. Monroe is the Ebenezer Scrooge of Evergreen Valley, Connecticut. If there was a building for sale or a penny on the street, he'd grab both.

"You know we're not interested in selling," I sigh, telling him for the tenth time this year.

"This place can't be bringing in much revenue. Let's say we double last month's sales on top of my offer for the building." He picks up a bookmark and drops it with a look of disgust. I don't know why he's in here again. I've made it perfectly clear I have no interest in selling this place. Not that it's mine to sell.

"No thanks." I shake my head and try to busy myself, hoping he'll take the hint and leave.

"You can't seriously be turning me down. Again. You have to know that it's silly to only sell one type of book—especially *romance* books." He scoffs, saying the word romance like it's disgusting. We're used to this kind of narrow-minded thinking around here. I try ignoring him, once again hoping he'll just drop it and leave.

"Where's your grandmother? Maybe she'll be a bit more reasonable than you." He looks around like she's hiding somewhere. Which, honestly, would be on brand for her. She's in her eighties and hates Mr. Monroe more than I do.

He's one of those obnoxiously handsome people that's used to getting things in life because of his looks. He got them from his father, who tried buying the bookstore from my grandmother years ago. Neither of us was impressed nor interested, and despite repeating that, they continued to try and offer us more money than we'd ever need.

"She's not here today, and I'm afraid if you continue with this, I'll have to ask you to leave," I say sharply with a customer service smile. I'm not in the mood to argue with him today.

"It's fine. I'm on my way out. But I'll be back." He shakes his head and heads out the front door with a jingle of the bells. A brush of cool November air flows through the shop.

"What's going on? What did he want this time?" My grandma comes out from the back office and takes her place behind the register, knitting a scarf for the holiday clothing drive.

"Mr. Monroe was just reminding us he wants the store. I turned him down, of course, and he asked for you." I sigh. It's nothing new.

"That man is even more persistent than his father." She scoffs.

She'd been the owner of Reading Into It since the late 70s. She opened the place with my grandfather. It was revolutionary back then, an all-romance bookstore. It was something that was almost unheard of, although now more common. Her parents thought it was a ridiculous idea, but with word of mouth and the tourist effect of our small town, she did well. Well enough to be open for almost fifty years. I've been working here since I was in high school, starting out part-time and moving up to manager after I got my bookkeeping degree in college. Eventually, this place will be mine, but for now my grandma and I share it. She can't quite do everything she used to, but she likes spending her days here anyway.

"I don't know why he thinks you'd change your mind after like, fifty years." I shake my head.

"Because the Monroe's have no brains. They only think in terms of money and business. All of them are as corrupt as the next," she says, grumbling. It's nothing new; I've heard this my entire life. The Monroes are greedy and wealthy, and they have never contributed to the community—unless by way of another apartment complex no one wanted.

"Don't let them raise your blood pressure," I warn her.

"Oh, I'm fine." She waves me off like she always does.

My grandma *is* fine for someone her age, but she needs to take it easy. She often pushes the limit of how much stress she should be taking on. But she tries to act like she's in her late twenties and not her late seventies.

Shaking my head, I go back to stacking the box of new releases by the register. We like to keep them next to the register because it's often what people came inside for. Sure, we have the tourists coming in to check out the place and buy bookish items. But the regulars come in like clockwork every Tuesday to pick up the new releases. So it helps having them right next to the register so they don't have to go looking for them. I stack the latest romances face-out so everyone can see the beautiful covers. I have a habit of buying a book because of the cover; it's like art for my shelf.

I should probably read more than I do. But between taking care of my grandma, the store, and having a life, reading has taken the back burner. Maybe I'll make it my new year's resolution to get back into it. It won't hurt to at least try. It's something I love, and it's relaxing, but I can't ever make time for it. Looking around at the empty store, I realize that it's a good time to read. I could sit in the back in case anyone needs me and just pick one of the new releases.

"Aren't you late to lunch with Parker? I can hold the fort down until the temp gets here," my grandma says, looking at the clock.

"Oh crap, yeah." I glance at my Apple watch. I guess I won't be doing any reading right now. Fighting with Mr. Monroe made time go by quickly. "And the temp's name is Andrea, please don't just call her the temp." I sigh. We hired someone to help out over the holidays, and today is her first shift after a week of training.

"Yeah, yeah, I'll write that down," she says, and I don't miss the sassy tone she has. I don't know what my grandma has against hiring temps, but she always gets grumpy about remembering their names.

"I'll see you later. Don't cause too much trouble," I tease and kiss her cheek chastely before I slip on my coat and head out the front door.

The winter chill hits me like a ton of bricks. It's so much fucking colder than I thought it was. I'm only walking down the road to Liz's Diner, but it's brisk enough to see my own breath. I drove in earlier and didn't even need my coat on. Now, I'm slipping on my gloves and pulling my hat down over my ears. My ears freezing is the disadvantage of my hair being cropped in the winter. Once my knitted green hat is pulled over my ears, I feel a little bit better. It helps that I'm late, so I'm rushing over instead of walking at a casual pace.

As soon as I'm across the street from the diner, I see my best friend's dark red hair through the window. She's seated at our favorite booth in the back and looking at a menu. That's not unusual for her. She gets something new every time we visit the diner, despite the menu never changing. I like to stick to my usual—a Diet Coke and grilled cheese. I tug open the heavy diner door, and the bells jingle above me.

"Hey Jax!"

A chorus of hellos greet me as I step inside.

Parker looks up and smiles as I tug off my coat and hang it on the coat rack by the doorway.

"Your usual?" Kate, one of the waitresses, asks. She's been working here since I was a kid.

"Yes please, thanks Kate." I smile.

"I didn't order yet. I wasn't sure if you were even coming," Parker says as I slip into the opposite side of the booth.

"Sorry, Mr. Scrooge stopped by the store, and I lost track of time." I sigh.

"Just say the word and I'll wipe his entire hard drive without any evidence," she says like it's no big deal. She's offered me this many times, but I always turn her down.

"I know you're a tech genius, but I don't want our weekly lunches to be in prison," I whisper, shaking my head.

"Fine." She shrugs.

"Do you know what you want, dear?" Kate asks, coming over with my Diet Coke.

"The Greek gyro with extra white sauce, a root beer, and fries please. Thanks, Kate," Parker says, handing over the menu.

"So, how's it going? Did anyone move into the house next door yet?" I ask. One of her neighbors moved out during the summer, and they haven't been able to find anyone to live there yet.

"Not yet. I still think you should take the place," Parker suggests.

"You know I can't. I like living with my grandma."

"You know she'd be fine if you moved out," Parker says, and despite me knowing she's right, I still can't.

"I just worry. What if I move out and something happens to her? I'd never forgive myself." I sigh.

"She wouldn't want you living your life like that if she knew you were staying for her," she insists.

"I know, but it's not like I'm dying to move out. I will eventually, but it's not on my radar right now." I shrug.

"Fine. I guess we can't be neighbors then." She feigns a sigh.

"I think that's for the best. If I saw you walking around your house naked, it would be too much Parker for me." I laugh.

"That's fair." She laughs.

We've been friends since middle school, and despite half the town thinking we're a couple, we've never even thought about crossing that line. It's like two queer women can't be friends without everyone assuming they've at least *done* it. But the truth is, I only see Parker as a sister—and my best friend. I can't even imagine thinking about them in a romantic way, and I know she feels the same. That's why the only time I saw her naked was when I accidentally forgot to knock and walked into her house using the key she gave me.

It's something I've never done again.

"Here you both are!" Kate drops off our food and Parker's drink.

"Thank you," we say in unison.

"Wait, so how did that first date go?" Parker asks, shoving a fry in her mouth.

"It didn't." I groan.

"Explain please," Parker says.

"She didn't show up. I waited twenty minutes then checked the app and she had unmatched me. I don't know what happened, but I got annoyed and just deleted the entire app," I admit.

"What? You can't give up that easily." She groans.

"Yes, I can. You told me to try online dating, and it was terrible."

"One not even date can't count!" she insists.

"It's fine. Maybe it's just not in the cards for me right now. I'm fine with that," I say. I've had my share of toxic and terrible relationships, so I don't mind being by myself.

"That's a damn shame. There's a masc shortage, apparently, and you're taking yourself out of the game." She shakes her head.

"You did *not* just say that." I start cracking up, and the Diet Coke I'm sipping almost comes out my nose.

"It's true! You know I usually fall for a hot femme but supposedly mascs are in short supply right now." Parker laughs.

"That's crazy."

"What's crazy is you acting like you don't have time for romance. Or at the very least, time to get laid. How sad is it that I know you haven't gotten laid in months?"

"It's creepy is what it is," I tease.

"I'm serious! It's the holiday season, and people are home for the holidays. We have tourists taking over the town, and you're not even trying. Promise me you'll come out for Shiloh's birthday at least," she insists.

"When is it?" I wince.

Parker rolls her eyes. "You're in the group chat. How can you not know when it is?"

"Maybe I muted it?" I wince again, knowing she's going to give me hell for that.

"Jax! You can't mute group chats! Then how will you know what's going on?"

"That's why I have you." I force a full smile. "Besides, it was going off way too much, so I decided to just mute it."

"Fine, whatever. Her birthday is next weekend. We're going out Saturday night to Teddy's Bar. There's a theme, too. You have to dress as your favorite holiday," Parker explains.

"Why is there a theme? Isn't she turning thirty?" I groan.

"So? You went to my Barbie themed twenty-fifth."

"Yes, I was a very convincing Ken. But that was almost five years ago, haven't we outgrown themed parties?" I ask, but Parker just stares at me. "Okay, got it. I'll pick a holiday."

"Not Valentine's Day, though, because that's mine. And I think Shiloh is going as Halloween. Seriously, you need to check the group chat." She cocks her head at me and looks toward my phone.

"Fine, fine. I'll unmute it later, I promise," I tell her. "Maybe

I'll go as Christmas. I don't know what other holiday I'd have something for." Maybe I could just find a Santa hat and throw it on. That counts as dressing up, right?

"That's the most obvious, considering Christmas is less than a month away. But you can't just throw on a Santa hat and call it a day," she says.

"Get out of my head! How did you know that's what I was thinking?" I frown.

"Because you're obvious, and my best friend. But actually put in an effort. Shiloh is inviting some of her college friends, and from what I hear, they're hot and single."

"Oh, joy," I say.

"Come on! I know it's been a while since you've dated anyone, but it's time to get back out there. Promise me you'll at least try?" Parker gives her signature puppy dog eyes. I don't know if it's because they're blue and big, but they always work on me no matter how much I don't want them to.

"Fine, I promise I'll try." I sigh.

"Yay! It'll be fun, and who knows? Maybe you'll actually meet someone!" She cheers.

I consider her words carefully; maybe it is about time I put myself out there again. I mean, it isn't like I'm going to meet the love of my life at home. Sure, they could walk into the bookstore, but that kind of thing only happens in movies or books.

Really cheesy movies and books.

THREE

El

It wasn't the first time I'd been in town, but it had been a long time since I'd been home. My parents love to think of this place as our home, but in reality, I spent most of my life trying to escape this small town. My parents didn't have the best reputation when I was growing up, and when it came to making friends, it didn't exactly make things easy on me. I was a bit of a homebody until I moved to the city for college and could actually make friends on my own. That's, in part, why I don't make it home as much as my parents would like. Of course my little sister, Paige, had the opposite experience. She loves the small-town life and never spent a day outside of this place.

"It's about time!" my sister says, running up to me. She wraps her arms around me in a tight hug, and I relax a bit.

"I said I was coming at noon," I say, confused. It isn't my fault that the train was a few minutes late. I can't drive, so I have to depend on other methods of transportation.

"I mean coming back to town. It's been years!"

"You know me—always working," I lie. Well, it isn't a total lie. I'm a successful real estate lawyer in the city, so it isn't like I can just drop things to come visit.

"Yeah yeah. Dad may fall for that, but I don't. Is this all you brought?" She looks at my small suitcase.

"Yes, as I told dad, I'll do what I can but I'm only staying the weekend," I say firmly. My parents have a habit of railroading me into things if I don't stand my ground.

"Is this about the bookstore?" Her tone turns sour.

"Yes, I thought Dad said you knew about it." I frown.

"Oh, I know all about it. He asked for my help, and I turned him down," Paige says before putting my suitcase in the trunk of her car.

"Why?" I ask as I slide in the passenger seat.

"Let's not fight about it. I'll let Dad explain everything. I'm just glad you're staying with me." She smiles.

"I am too." I'm curious about what she isn't telling me, but my meeting with Dad is at one o'clock, so I don't have to wait too long for answers.

"Dad is waiting for you at the office in town. I figured we'd drop off your stuff first and then head there?" she suggests.

"Sounds good. You're the boss."

Paige goes on about the new job she got at the local library. She's been working there for years as she finished her librarian degree, but now that she graduated, she's officially a librarian. With her head always in the books, it's no surprise to me. I was just surprised she never ventured away from Evergreen Valley. She has an adventurous personality—as long as she's within a small radius of home.

We pull up to her apartment she shares with a few friends from college. They all have their own space but share a living space. Since her bedroom is the biggest, she doesn't mind sharing with me for the weekend. It will be like when we were kids and we'd pull her mattress into my room for a night or two. We'd sneak snacks and stay up all night talking—until I ulti-mately fell asleep.

"Crap, Dad wants to see you now. I'll run your stuff inside and bring you right over." Paige sighs.

"Okay, do you want help?"

"Are you crazy? No way, you're a guest." She waves me off.

Five minutes later, she's back in the car, and we're headed to the other side of town. Our father's office is in one of the buildings next to the bank. He owns the entire building but rents out the offices to different people throughout it. As we pull up, I realize nothing has really changed. The town looks just as small as usual, and the buildings don't even look like they've gotten so much as a cleaning. I tug my jacket closed, remembering we're farther north than I'm used to.

"Eliora! Thank goodness you're here," my father greets me with open arms.

"Hey, Dad." I force a smile as I return his hug.

"Paige, I didn't think you were coming." He frowns at my sister.

"I'm not staying. I just wanted to make sure El got here okay. I'll pick you up later, unless Dad wants to give you a ride," Paige says.

"I'll text you," I say. We don't need to decide right now. I'll see how this meeting goes.

"Sounds good." Paige gives me a quick hug goodbye, and I follow Dad into his office.

"Have a seat. You can look over all the documents we have."

"All of them?" I raise an eyebrow.

"It's not that many." He chuckles. "It's mainly the lease Ms. Evans has. I also printed the laws in Connecticut about leases since I know you primarily practice in New York. You'll also find any other miscellaneous items I thought might come in handy. We're basically looking for a way to get her out of this lease— we've offered to buy her out and she refused. So now we have to do it the hard way."

"Any idea why Grandpa wants this building so bad?" I ask, even though I sort of know the answer.

"You know what he always says. It's the corner building and could be great for a hotel—or something bigger, considering we now own the two buildings right next door as well," he explains.

I take the paperwork and look it over. There's some stuff my father highlighted and some things that are a little different from New York laws. But it's also not my first time dealing with Connecticut laws. A lot of my clients have properties in other states, and I have to stay up to date on the basic laws. Everything seems pretty standard, until I get to one spot.

"They didn't pay their mortgage on time," I point out.

"What?" He grabs his copy of the paperwork and realizes I'm right.

"It's been late the last three months. It hasn't been paid at all in December. It says that the owner of the building gave her an extension. But didn't you mention that he died?"

"Yes, at the beginning of last month. That's how I became the legal owner of the building, but I haven't found a legal way to remove her from the premises." My father raises an eyebrow.

"Then, technically, since the extension wasn't in writing, it's not legal. She's past due for the mortgage, and if you want to, you can serve her with an eviction notice. She'd have thirty days to put up the funds for the missed mortgage, and in truth, you could also have her pay the extra interest rate for all the days she's late. That would almost double the costs," I explain.

"Holy shit, Eliora, that's amazing." He picks up his phone and starts telling his assistant to draw up the official papers and get the eviction notice started.

While he's going back and forth with his assistant about all the specifics, I check my phone. Tara wasn't thrilled that I took a last-minute trip home. And she was less thrilled when I told her I didn't want her to come with me. It wasn't about my family; they'd met her before. It was about not getting stuck here longer than I wanted to be. Tara would want to do family dinners and stay at a hotel or something, and I don't have time for that. I want to fix this for my father and get back to the city as quick as possible. But of course, she hasn't replied to the many texts I sent her while I was on the train. I even sent her a DoorDash delivery of her favorite sushi, but according to the Ring camera, it's still sitting in the hallway—untouched.

"Can you bring this over? I would do it myself, but this is going to put me behind on so many things," my father says.

"Bring what?" I look as he drops the official eviction notice on my lap.

"It's right across the street. You can have your sister pick you up, right?" I can't help but get the feeling I'm getting the boot. I helped and now I'm done with what I was needed for here.

"Sure." I grab my things, not wanting to kick a gift horse in the mouth.

I tighten my coat around my waist and put my gloves back on as I walk down the street past the bank, cross at the light, and stop in front of the bookstore. It's a little run down, the sign looks to be the original from when the place first opened, what, almost fifty years ago? I can see why. I know they don't have the funds to update it. Why won't they just let the place go? I'm sure my father offered them enough money to start over somewhere else.

I walk inside, the door jingling above me as I look around. The inside is cute; all the walls are painted a muted pink, and there are white bookshelves that look vintage. There are books everywhere, and the shelves are labeled according to subgenre. As I start to look around, I remember I'm here on official business and it wouldn't look too good for me to be shopping here. I'm not much of a reader anyway. I head to the front register and look at the woman who can't be older than twenty-one.

"Excuse me, is the owner here?" I ask, glancing at her name tag—Andrea.

"Uh yeah, Jax?" Andrea calls, and I turn my attention toward the person she called over.

My jaw almost drops—the woman walking toward me is not who I expected at all. Jax and I had gone to high school together but it wasn't like I knew what she looked like. I had kept to myself and blocked out most memories from high school. This woman is several inches taller than my five-six, with short, dark, curly hair. It's cropped and there are perfectly arranged ringlets around her face. Her face is full of soft features, no makeup that I can see, and she has dark eyebrows and pale pink lips. She has an array of earrings along the outside of her ear on one side, but otherwise no jewelry. She's thin, wearing a black sweater and a pair of khakis. She is absolutely beautiful, and if I had met her under any other circumstance, I'd be asking for her number.

"Can I help you?" she asks, breaking my focus. My mouth forms a hard line as I switch into work mode.

"Are you Ms. Evans?" I ask.

"I'm her granddaughter, but she's not in today. Can I ask what this is about?" She crosses her arms and studies me intently. I wonder if she knows who I am—we were only a few years apart in school, but it wasn't like I made a point of being social in this town.

"I'm here on behalf of Monroe Industries. This is an official eviction notice. You have thirty days to come up with the funds listed here or vacate the premises." I hand her the paper, and she scans it. She's trying to think of something to say, but I turn around. I did what I came to do, and I don't need to stick around and see her cry.

"Wait!" She catches my arm, and I gasp quietly. Her eyes meet mine, dark orbs matching her curls.

"Yes?" I ask, sharply.

"There has to be something we can do. There's no way we can pay this much so soon. You have to work with us here," she pleads.

As much as I want to help her, I owe it to my father to stay in work mode. "I'm sorry but the eviction notice is official. My father offered to buy out your lease. I can maybe see if that's still on the table. But I doubt it, considering the state of the mortgage."

"Your father?" She scoffs. She must connect the dots on who I am, because she looks me over and her face contorts to anger.

"Mr. Monroe, of Monroe Industries. I'm Eliora Monroe. I'm sorry this is the way we're meeting." I extend my hand as I would toward any client, but she just stares at me until I drop it. "Anyway, you have thirty days. If you need anything further, you can contact my father."

"How can your family do this?" she asks angrily.

"My family isn't doing anything but collecting on a property they should rightfully own," I say.

"You do realize my grandmother has owned this place for almost fifty years, right? This is her business and livelihood?" Jax growls.

"That's not Monroe Industries' concern. We're looking for the owed mortgage and the interest it accrued," I say, keeping my tone steady. This is common; people get upset when it's personal. It's important that I don't engage in it or say anything incriminating at this point.

"You know you sound like a robot, right? Do you even care about the people you're hurting, or do you just do it for the money like your family?" She scoffs.

I don't say anything. I turn to go, but Jax stops to grab something off the shelf. It seems to calm her, and for a brief second, I'm afraid she's going to throw it at me. But instead, she walks closer to me and extends the book toward me.

"I think you should read this. Maybe it'll give you a glimpse into what we've been trying to do here. If not, you might at least see who I'll be comparing you to from now on." She hands me the book, and surprisingly, I take it.

Before she says anything else, I leave out the front door. What does she think a book is going to do? I'd read it and convince my father to drop the eviction process? This isn't some Hallmark movie. I scoff and almost throw the book in the trash can outside, but something stops me. Who is she going to be comparing me to? Is there some main character that I remind her of? Curiosity gets the better of me, so when I get to Paige's apartment, I still have the book. And for some reason, I tuck it into my suitcase for safekeeping. Not that I ever intend to read the thing, but for some reason, I can't get rid of it either. The way Jax looked at me before she knew who I was lingers in my head.

Thank God I'm not staying for the holidays. Being attracted to Jax Evans would be the worst thing I could do in my family's eyes. Being gay, they can accept, but this? There's no way anyone would forgive me, so I push the thought of it away to some forgotten part of my mind—for safekeeping.

FOUR

Jax

The moment Eliora leaves the store, I retreat to the office, slamming the door shut. I see red—how the hell can she waltz in here with her four-inch heels and hand me an eviction notice like it's nothing? I know the Monroes are hardcore, but I've never experienced it firsthand. They are dismantling the town property by property. And that daughter of his? Walking in here like she doesn't have a care in the world? Resting bitch face along with her too-rich clothing and bored expressions.

Eliora and I went to high school together, but I don't think we ever spoke to each other. She was a few years younger than I am and a bit of a wallflower. I don't recall her being around much for any school functions, and I was at all of them. She is different than I remember her, carrying herself with more confidence and grace. I remember her being picked on for being overweight in high school, but she carries her curves confidently now.

I push the office chair hard into the wall. The sound vibrates across the floor, and a few picture frames shake, but nothing falls. Sighing, I put the chair back where it belongs and look at the eviction notice. On the front it is clear—thirty days to clear out. But on the back, there is a bunch of legal nonsense I don't understand. Does my grandma really owe that much money? I thought we were all caught up on our bills. How has it gotten this out of hand?

"Jax? Uh, sorry to bother you, but I don't know how to do a gift card sale," Andrea says, poking her head in.

"Okay, I'll be right there." I sigh, putting the notice on my desk.

Putting on my best customer service smile, I force myself to help people until the day is over. I can't let my own emotions take over the day—especially when this might be the last time I get to do this. I can't even think about it, just knowing how devastated my grandma is going to be. By the time we're closing up, I'm racing home to tell her. She's not the best with cell phones, and this is the kind of news you need to deliver in person.

As soon as I walk inside, I smell fresh marinara sauce, chicken cutlets, and pasta cooking. An array of spices fills my nose, and I relax as I take off my jacket and boots. I drop my keys in the basket by the door and head for the kitchen to wash my hands.

"Oh! You're home early! I thought you were doing sales for next week?" my grandma says, surprised. I place a kiss on her cheek and grab a glass of water.

"I'm going out later for Shiloh's birthday, but I wanted to stop home to see you before I change," I say.

"Well, dinner has five more minutes, and then you can eat before you go. You're all skin and bones." My grandma always chastises me for not eating enough, even though I'm perfectly healthy for my height.

"I need to tell you something first." I sigh, sitting at the kitchen table.

"What?" She raises an eyebrow as she brings the sauce spoon to her lips, pauses, and adds another dash of something.

"The Monroes came by today—"

She huffs. "Oh great, what did he want?"

"No, it wasn't Mr. Monroe. It was his daughter, Eliora. She came by with an eviction notice, and as much as I don't want to believe it, it's legit. We have thirty days to come up with all the money they're asking for, plus interest and late fees," I explain, putting the paper on the table.

"You know I can't read that without my glasses." She waves the paper away.

"Why didn't you tell me we were behind on things? I could've helped."

"No. This isn't your responsibility." She waves me off.

"It's going to be my responsibility if our livelihood is compromised by this," I say softly. I'm trying not to get angry with her, but I can't for the life of me understand why she didn't tell me what was going on.

"It's not as bad as it seems, and I am taking care of it."

"It's almost fifteen grand, Grandma. I don't have that kind of money lying around. Do you?" I exclaim.

"Obviously not, or I would have paid it." She mumbles over the food.

The timers go off, and she shuts them off as she begins draining the pasta. I grab plates from the cabinet, then silverware from the drawer, and sit back down. She quietly places food on our plates and sits across from me. It's times like these I wish my parents were still around. They died in a car accident when I was too young to remember them, and since then it's been me and Grandma. My grandpa was around for most of my childhood until he died my first year of high school. He got sick and then he was gone.

My grandma never lets us feel too sad about the people we lost. We grieve them, and every year on the anniversary of their deaths, we have their favorite foods in their honor. Lasagna for my grandpa. Pizza for my parents. And for the most part, I'm fine. But it's times like this, when I'm forced to be older than I should be—forced to be the grown-up and fix this so we're not jobless as well as homeless—that it bothers me.

My grandma doesn't say another word about the bookstore throughout dinner, so I don't bring it up again. I get changed and head out to meet Parker before we go to Shiloh's birthday thing. Parker usually likes to be the designated driver, so I am spending the night at their house.

"Didn't I tell you that you can't just wear a Santa hat?" Parker teases as I step out of my car.

"I'm literally wearing a coat because it's five degrees out. I have a Christmas sweater on under this." I laugh.

"Fine." She unlocks the door to her car, and I check out her outfit—a sweater dress covered in pink and red hearts, red over-the-knee boots, and her makeup done with pink hearts on her cheeks.

"You certainly went all out," I say.

"I'm convinced this is my time. You never know who you will meet," she says as she drives toward the bar, which is conveniently located next to the town's firehouse.

"I just want to get as drunk as possible tonight," I say.

"Are you okay?" She looks at me warily. I'm not normally someone who gets drunk too often.

I sigh, not knowing where to start, but I tell Parker about my run-in with bitch-face Monroe.

"So now we have thirty days, and I don't know what the hell we can do," I explain.

"I mean, I probably have some money in my savings I could lend you. But most of my money is tied up in the house." Parker frowns.

"No, thank you, but no. I want to figure this out in a way that doesn't leave us terribly indebted to anyone else."

"That makes sense. Although I definitely wouldn't charge you interest on it." Parker laughs.

A knock on the window causes us both to jump. Shiloh and some friends are standing outside the bar dressed as different holidays. Shiloh has on an orange crop top with a jack-o'-lantern face cut out and a black mini skirt. Her friends are dressed as the

Fourth of July and Easter—one of them in an American flag dress and the other in a bunny onesie.

"It's about time! We pre-gamed without you!" Shiloh cheers as we greet everyone.

"I guess I'll have to catch up then," I tease as I follow them inside.

Teddy's is a small-town dive bar. We've known the three bartenders since we've been old enough to come in. When we had fakes and wanted anything, we had to head into the next town over. Now that we're of age, we take advantage of their $6 shots and $5 drinks. Shiloh orders a round of vodka shots with my vodka Sprite. We toss them back, then she leads everyone over to the dance floor—the back part of the bar with no chairs or tables, closest to the largest speaker.

"Jax, these are my friends from college! I don't think you guys have met yet, but this is Chrissy, Macy, and Jane." She introduces me to Easter, Fourth of July, and what I assume is New Year's with the sparkly dress and champagne headband.

"Nice to meet y'all, I'm Jax." I shake each of their hands politely, and as much as I want to feel a spark or at least be interested in these beautiful women, I'm not. The only thing on my mind is Eliora Monroe.

Parker hands me another drink as she sips on her Diet Coke, and I toss it back. I am not going to let this woman ruin my night. Three drinks and a lot of dancing later, I have to pee and make my way to the ladies' room. An older woman gives me a weird look, like I'm not in the right place—which is unfortunately something I'm used to. Whenever they see butch-presenting women, they think we're confused or something.

As I'm washing my hands, a blonde fixing her hair bumps into me and immediately apologizes. It's why I love the ladies' room when we're drunk—everyone is so nice to each other and is having a good time. I stop at the bar for another drink before I return to the group.

"We're doing shots, so catch up," Shiloh tells me and shoves a shot glass in my hand.

I toss back what I think is tequila and wince. That isn't my drink of choice, but I suppose it will have to do. I'm already drunk, the room and Jax have a nice haze, and I feel more relaxed than I was earlier. Whoever is in charge of the music tonight is playing an early 2000s playlist, which keeps us in a good mood. We're all dancing and singing along to the music when a man comes to flirt with Shiloh. She likes everyone, so I don't immediately do anything—until she's yelling at him. One moment everything is fine, the next there's a drink being thrown in his face, and he's storming off.

"What the hell just happened?" I yell to Parker.

"He asked if he could help us celebrate the holidays on his face," Shiloh explains.

"What a freaking tool bag. Guys think they can just say and do anything." I scoff.

"It's annoying, but it's fine. No need to get so worked up over some guy." Shiloh shrugs it off.

But I'm too angry and tired of holding it in. I storm after the man Shiloh just covered in a drink, shoving his shoulder to get his attention.

"What the fuck?" he yells, turning around. "Who even are you?"

"You said some shitty stuff to my friend," I say angrily.

"Yeah, and she threw her drink at me. I could sue her for that —she's lucky it didn't blind me," he says dramatically.

Parker appears next to me—or maybe she's always been there—but she's pulling on my shoulder, trying to get my attention off this man. I shrug her off and step closer to him.

"You're lucky that's all she did. You can't go around talking to women like that! You can't just say whatever the hell you want and think everything will be fine!" I yell.

"Jax, come on." Parker pulls me back, but I shrug her off again.

"Oh great, I stumbled upon a group of feminists," he says, rolling his eyes, as if that word is the worst insult he can think of.

"You're so lucky I don't kick your ass for the way you spoke to my friend tonight," I grumble before letting Parker pull me back to the group.

"What the hell has gotten into you?" Parker asks. I'm not usually the confrontational type, but I'm tired of being pushed around today. Tired of the ones I care about being hurt by assholes who think they can do whatever they want.

"I'm just so sick of men like that—and women too. Like, who the fuck do people think they are to act like there are no consequences in life?" I say angrily.

"Is this about the store?" Parker asks softly.

"Of course it is! How the hell can the Monroes give us thirty days for eviction? And at Christmastime?! It's just cruel" I yell.

"You're being evicted?" Shiloh asks, eyes wide.

"I'm sorry, I didn't want to ruin your party by bringing it up. But yeah, they came by today with the papers," I explain.

"Is there anything you can do?" she asks.

"Not unless you can come up with fifteen grand by New Year's." I sigh.

"There has to be something we can do," Parker adds.

"What if you had a fundraiser?" Shiloh suggests.

"Like a bake sale or something?" I scoff.

"No, like a holiday party or something that could bring the town together but also raise the money?" Shiloh says.

Parker looks at me just as lightbulbs in my head begin to go off. We could throw a party—I'm sure with the connections I have in town we could all come together and figure something out. I'm not going to ask anyone for their money, but if I'm giving them something, then it doesn't seem so bad. Evergreen Valley used to have an annual holiday party, but the Monroes put a stop to it when they bought the old wedding reception hall. With nowhere to host it, it sort of fell through the cracks.

But what if I can find somewhere to host it and actually pull this off?

"Would we have enough time to plan this?" I ask nervously, looking between Parker and Shiloh.

"A sane person wouldn't, but we're not sane. We're going to do everything we can to make sure you and your grandma don't lose Reading Into It," Parker says with a reassuring smile.

"We have to get brainstorming. Parker, start taking notes, and Shiloh, we're going to need some more shots," I say.

Maybe this is all a drunken plan that won't amount to anything in the morning. But at least I feel like I'm doing something. I can't do nothing while the family business falls apart. It was hard enough seeing Grandma so upset tonight. I can't imagine if she doesn't have the store to visit every day and her legacy living on when she eventually passes.

FIVE

El

"You've got to be kidding me, El," Paige says after I explained what happened this afternoon.

"What?" I look at her, confused.

"That bookstore is older than dad. You can't seriously tell me you're on board with his ridiculous plan to take it over?" She frowns, her plump lips forming a thick line.

"I have absolutely no ties to this town like that, P. I'm just here as a favor to Dad," I say. "Besides, what's the difference to you? It's not like you work there or are even friends with the owners."

"So? I have basic empathy, which seems to be something Dad —and now you—are lacking. This woman is in her late seventies? Maybe eighties? And you just walk over there and basically handed her a death sentence." Paige is pacing around the living room—as she often does when she's stressed.

"I have empathy, but maybe it's time for her to retire. If she would've taken Dad up on one of his deals, then she'd be able to have a cushy retirement. Maybe I can see if Dad is willing to offer her another way out."

"Like what?" Paige stops.

"Like maybe we can buy them out and they'd make a profit

instead of losing everything. Now they know we're serious. Sometimes we do that with clients who won't let go of something. It's a risky bluff and you have to be willing to follow through but it could work," I say, thinking about some of my past clients this has worked for.

"You've got to be kidding me!" Paige throws her arms up in the air.

"What?"

"You sound just like Dad, you know. And I know you once told me that's your worst nightmare, so can you tell me how the hell that happened? Because I definitely do not want that to happen to me," she says.

"I'm not like Dad," I say quietly.

"Yes, you are. You don't see these people for what they are, you're just looking at them as pawns and money," Paige snaps.

I go silent, unsure of what to say. I don't want to fight with her, and I know I've gotten a little tougher since I went into law. But that's part of the job. You need a strong backbone to be successful in this field. I fight for my clients more than I've ever fought for myself. Sure, a lot of my work is divorced clients or families fighting over estates, but that's what I'm good at.

"I just don't like seeing you like this. I know Dad was upset you didn't follow in his footsteps to take over the business, but by acting just like him you may as well have." She sighs and heads down the hall to her room, slamming the door shut behind her.

I feel awkward, being in her living room without her. Only one of her roommates is home, but they've made themselves scarce since we got here. Not knowing what else to do, I pull out my phone and check for any other updates. Tara had finally picked up the DoorDash I left her, but since it was soggy from the snow—and frozen—she threw it right in the trash. I decide maybe I should talk to her. A phone call might be better than trying to get through over text.

"Hello?" Tara picks up on the third ring.

"Hey babe, how are you?" I take it as a good sign she picked up the phone.

"El, are you serious right now?" She scoffs.

"Come on, I thought things would be okay by now." I sigh.

"You thought you'd take off randomly before the holidays, without me, and then I'd just be fine with it?" Tara says angrily.

"I understand you're upset—"

"No, you don't get that I'm upset. You try to fix things with food I don't eat and flowers I don't even like."

"I thought you loved sushi."

"I haven't eaten sushi since I got food poisoning three months ago. But it's not like you'd know that because you're never home," she grumbles.

"You know I have a demanding job."

"But yet somehow you can take a weekend off at the drop of a hat if your father asks?" She's waiting for me to tell her she's wrong, and I hate that I can't.

"It's not like my father asks for much. This was important to my family."

"Am I important to you?" Her question catches me off guard.

"What?"

"Am I important to you? It should be a fairly simple question to answer about someone you've been dating for the last several years," Tara insists.

"You are." I sigh. I hate how forced this feels. Like I have to constantly prove that I love her and the way I show it isn't enough.

"Are we fooling ourselves by pretending this is still working? I don't even know if I'm important to you or if you're seeing a future here anymore," Tara says.

"Is that how you really feel?" I ask. I'm not entirely caught off guard. Deep down, I knew this was coming.

"Maybe we should take another break. It seemed to do us some good last time." Tara sighs.

"Break or break up?" We've done our fair share of both over the last few years.

"Is there a difference?"

"Am I coming home to you this weekend or am I going to find you suddenly moved out? Are you going to be seeing what else is out there or trying to mend things between us?" I ask.

"I'll be here for now, but I don't know how much longer I can do this. I love you El, but I wish you loved me more than work," Tara whispers.

"Work is a lot on me right now, but things should clear up in the new year and then we should be okay."

"Yeah, I've heard that before, El. I just don't know if it's worth waiting for anymore." Tara sighs.

"Okay."

We hang up without saying *I love you*, which isn't uncommon. I can't recall the last time we said it where it wasn't over text. I don't know the last time we kissed, let alone had sex, and I'd be lying if I said I missed it. Tara is my first serious, adult relationship, and sometimes I wonder if this is how things are supposed to be. We've been together for so long that we went down the checklist doing all the things long-term couples do. It's less about how we feel and more about what we think we should be doing. But then I see my sister living with roommates, working at her dream job and not even thinking about settling down, and I wonder if that's something I've missed out on.

I've never been someone who wants to spend every night at a bar, but it would be nice to feel something more than complacency. The last time I felt any type of spark with someone was when I saw Jax. Aside from Jax's beauty, there was something about her that captured my attention. I wanted to hang on her every word and get to know her. Which of course, I can't. It's stupid. I'm probably misreading this spark as Jax's hatred for me. She was shooting daggers at the back of my head as I left the bookstore.

"Come on. Mom asked us to come over for dinner tonight," Paige says, coming down the stairs in a different outfit.

"Is that a good idea?" I ask.

"Probably not, but I wasn't going to give them a chance to be upset with me. I'm used to being the black sheep on the daily." She sighs.

I slide my boots and coat back on, following Paige to her car. She drives us to the edge of town, where our parents live in an oversized house. It's way too big for just the two of them, but they have help to keep it looking spotless. In high school, when Paige had friends over, we had enough spare bedrooms that no one ever had to share. My fists tighten as we walk up the long path, and my chest feels heavy with each step. I don't remember the last time I was home and actually visited this house.

"Eliora! You look amazing! It's so great to see you!" My mother greets us with hugs, which surprises me. My mother has never been much of a hugger.

"Your father is so happy to have you home. We made some of your favorites—chicken stir fry and double chocolate cake for dessert. Well, I didn't make it, the chef did, but I swear it's delicious." My mother smiles.

"Sounds great." I smile, not mentioning that chicken stir fry hasn't been my favorite in over a decade.

"Come on in. It's just about ready, so we can have a seat." My mother ushers us in after we take off our coats and shoes by the door.

"Wine? We have red and white, but I'm afraid I don't know which you prefer." My mother frowns.

"Red is fine, thank you." I smile.

She pours three glasses and hands one to me and my sister before taking hers and sitting at the head of the table. My sister and I take our seats on opposite sides, our unspoken assigned seats since we were kids. Then my father comes in a moment later, *smiling*.

"There she is! I just got off the phone with your grandfather, and I can't tell you how happy he is that you've helped solve our little problem! He said there's an extra bonus being added to his will as we speak," my father praises.

"Thanks, Dad," I say shyly. Paige shifts in her seat. I can tell she's trying not to say anything.

"Marie, I'm serious. This is amazing news. Our daughter is going to make my father so happy. Something I couldn't even do," he says happily to my mother.

"Can we talk about something else?" Paige asks.

"What? Why? You should be just as happy!" my father says.

My sister lets go of all the tension she'd been holding back. "I should be happy you're destroying a family's business? Something that's been around longer than you? That my family is the one doing the destroying?"

"Paige," my mother says softly, but the tone she uses is a warning.

"No. I'm serious. How could he think I would be *just as happy*?" she adds in a mocking tone.

"Because this is a win for the family—this is a win for *us*. You know your grandfather has been trying to acquire this property his entire life and has been unsuccessful. Because of your sister, we finally have the chance we need to get it," my father says angrily.

"But at what cost?" Paige asks.

"Besides, without the bookstore, I'm sure you'll have a gaggle of new library patrons. And that's great for the community," he adds.

"Most readers already have library cards, Dad. It's not like we'll be helping them. If anything, we'll be contributing to the masses finding books on the dreaded online stores," she says angrily.

"Maybe we should change the subject," my mother says.

"Of course, because why would we want to talk about how our family is actively hurting the community?" Paige says.

"I just don't think your sister or I should have to sit through this. It's fine for you to disagree, but what's done is done," my father says sharply.

Paige opens her mouth to say something but just as quickly closes it and sits quietly. We start eating the food the chef placed in front of us—silently. My mother and father talk about the upcoming holiday plans, and my sister sits in silence. I can see something happening behind her eyes. She's planning and plotting something, but I can't be sure what exactly. I wouldn't put it past her to go against my father. She's never done so publicly, but she isn't shy about standing up for herself against him in private. Maybe she's at the point where she doesn't care about public perceptions of the Monroe's anymore. It wouldn't surprise me, but it would throw my father into a fit. It's very likely something he'd cut her off for.

The rest of dinner, I sit mumbling answers to questions I'm only half paying attention to. This feels like my life lately. At work, with Tara, with my family—all I have are complacent relationships and do what's expected of me. I don't push the envelope or question what's going on. I want to get through life peacefully, but at what cost? I'm exhausted by feeling so stuck and silent in my life. It doesn't seem to matter to anyone what I actually think or feel about the situations. I'm just there as another body, or so it seems. I'm not sure what I could even do to change that.

As much as it's hard to see my little sister fight with my dad, I'm jealous of her. It's so easy for her to stand up for what she believes in, even if it's against everyone else. She never questions if she should be on another side, she just does what she thinks is right. I'm jealous of the bad-assery that she exudes. Maybe I need to be more like her—if only I knew what I wanted to fight for. I don't have it in me to fight against my father, even if I don't believe entirely in his cause. There are generations of work in progress, and I don't want to interfere with that.

I wish it would come naturally to me to speak up instead of being a bystander. Being home just takes me back to high school when I was a wallflower at every event and barely noticed by anyone. I went to my classes, never raised my hand, and went home. Sometimes I thought about doing or being more, but I didn't want the pressure that came with it. It was easier just sticking to what I knew, keeping my head down until I moved to the city. I had always thought once I moved, I'd be able to be more of myself. And sure, I had been in college for a while. But now it was like I had forgotten that part of myself.

As I look at my little sister, quietly plotting something, I make a plan to promise to find the version of myself that will be myself. That I won't just take up space in places that I am in, but instead find spaces I *want* to be in. I take a big gulp of my wine— the idea terrifies me, to say the least. But I'm relieved I'm *feeling* something for once.

SIX

Jax

I t turns out, even when we're drunk, my friends and I are extremely smart. Although it's a bunch of notes on bar napkins and in my Notes app, there is a solid start to a plan. So within three days, Shiloh, Parker, and I have put together a flyer looking for more volunteers to help. My grandmother thinks it's a waste of time for the inevitable, but that doesn't stop me from trying. Parker and I set up a sign-up sheet in the store, and people have been coming in all day to offer help and ideas. A lot of my regulars have showed up, but with Shiloh putting out the word of the Monroes being behind this, a lot of the town has come by too. No one wants to see another business be taken over by Mr. Monroe and his family.

I'm putting books on the shelf when I notice one of my regulars come in. I'm not sure what her name is, but I've seen her come in quite often, especially when there is a new romance release she wants. I think she's a few years younger than me, but other than that, I don't know much. She's polite but keeps to herself when she is here.

"Can I help you?" I look at the short brunette with a perky smile.

"I'm Paige, and I'm hoping to help you. I heard you're still looking for help with the fundraiser for the bookstore, and I think I can help," Paige says.

"How's that?" Something about her seems familiar, but I can't quite put my tongue on it.

"The library has a rec room that would be perfect for the holiday party. It's almost never used, and it's indoors, and I've run it by my boss, and they're happy to help with whatever you need." She smiles.

"Really?" My eyes light up; I can't hide my excitement. Finding a venue is proving to be one of the hardest problems.

"I have all the paperwork here; she just needs your information. That way, in case you guys need anything or she has questions, you can be in contact." She hands me a stack of papers, and I glance at the top. That's when it stops me.

"You're Paige Monroe? Is this some kind of a joke?" I ask angrily.

"What? No. I mean, yes, I am a Monroe, but it's not a joke." She scrambles defensively.

"Nice try. Was this all some kind of ploy to see us fail? Maybe have us plan the whole thing, and at the last minute the library pulls out and we have nowhere to go? I'm not falling for that." I shake my head angrily.

"No! I swear." Paige races after me. "My last name is Monroe, yes. But I do not agree with my father or anything he's doing. My sister either. I've tried talking to both of them, and it's useless, but I can't not do anything."

"I can't work with someone I don't trust." I cross my arms over my chest.

"I understand, so work with my boss until you trust me. I've always loved this bookstore, and I would hate to see it disappear just to become another Starbucks or something."

My jaw drops. "Is that what he's doing with it?"

"No, no, I have no idea. I'm just saying. I don't want this place to go anywhere." She frowns.

"You have to understand my hesitation." I sigh, looking her over.

"I do. I can't change my last name or my family, but I'm here. I'm trying. Just take my boss's card and talk directly with them. If you decide to trust me, I'm happy to help out with whatever else you need. If you don't, well, I understand." Paige hands me a business card for the director of the Evergreen Public Library, Dawn Young.

"Okay, thank you." I take the card, unsure if I'll actually use it or not.

"I'm sorry. You know what they say—you can't choose your family." Paige offers a half smile before leaving.

"What was that about?" Parker asks as I walk over to where she's using the bookstore's printer to print out more flyers for the event.

"That was Paige Monroe. I guess the youngest of the kids."

Parker's eyebrows bunch together. "What did she want?"

"To help. She offered the library's rec room as a space for the event."

"You're not going to take her up on it, are you?" She looks surprised.

"I don't know. She gave me her boss's information, said she doesn't even have to be involved in any way. I feel suspicious, but we also really need a place that can host us for free." I grimace.

"I would vet her and then check it out again," Parker says.

"I know. I'll put it down as a maybe; I don't want to put this thing together and then we lose out because we've been played," I say.

"So, not to change the subject, but I was thinking. Not everyone can donate money, but what if at the party we did a silent auction? And all the local businesses could donate like a basket or a gift card to their place?" Parker suggests.

"Holy shit, I love that. It would be a great way to help out

everyone in the community while also raising funds for us."
I nod.

"That's what I was thinking, so I created these too. I thought
we could walk them over to everyone and explain the situation
in person. It's a lot harder to say no to someone in need if they're
looking you in the eye," Parker adds.

"Why the hell did you go into cybersecurity? You clearly
have an eye for business."

"Cybersecurity is where the money is. How else do you think
I could afford a house before I'm thirty?" She laughs.

"Okay, fair."

"Do you want to come with me to talk to people? Or do you
need to stay here?" Parker asks.

"I need to stay here, at least until Andrea comes in later. My
grandma hasn't been coming by the store lately." I sigh.

"She still hasn't been by since the eviction notice went up?"
Parker frowns.

"No. She thinks it's over for us and doesn't want to see it. I
keep trying to convince her there's a way out of it, but it's almost
like she's already given up." It's frustrating, but it's not like I can
argue with her about it.

"I'm sorry. I know how much this place means to the two of
you. I promise we'll do everything we possibly can to save the
place." Parker offers me a half smile.

I just nod, unsure of what else I can say that hasn't been said
already. I'm doing everything I can to keep the place open while
also raising the funds to keep it going past the eviction notice. I
haven't seen the Monroes' daughter, Eliora, since that day, but
she's been on my mind. Why does someone who looks like that
have to be related to my enemy? Have to *be* one of my enemies?
How the hell is Paige so different than her sister? Is she adopted?

I have a checklist of things to do before Andrea comes in
later, so once Parker heads out, I get to work. I'm hanging the
holiday lights in the window like I do every year when I hear the
local kids come by. I step off the ladder to say hi.

"Jax! Are you coming to the snowball fight tomorrow?" one of the local kids, Tommy, asks.

"Of course!" I smile.

Whenever there's a big snow that puts them out of school, or on a weekend, they gather in town for a snowball fight. Any kid is welcome as long as they stay warm. We head to Liz's diner afterward for free cocoa and whatever snacks are left over from the day before. Parents of the younger kids come, and older kids bring their siblings. Some parents choose to stay nearby at the diner, but most of the time it is the same group of kids who choose to come.

"Kate says she's got marshmallows with our names on it for after," Andy adds cheerfully.

"I think there might be an extra one in store for the winner." I wink. All the kids start chattering and gasping.

"See you tomorrow! Don't be late!" Tommy smiles, and he walks with his friends down toward the park.

Once they're safely across the street, I step back on the ladder. It is cold today, but it's not too bad out. I don't expect more snow, but maybe it won't be too bad. The lights hang just above the window, which I need to get painted. I usually do some kind of a mural around the window so people can still see in and see the window display of books. I haven't given it much thought yet this year because I'm too worried about keeping the place open.

The lights are hung, so I take the ladder back inside to the storage closet and get working on the displays inside. Right now, we have several themed shelves up, including "When Your Ex Returns for the Holidays," "Small Town Holidays," "Snowed-Inn," "Winter Holidays (That Aren't Christmas)," "Only One Bed—Holiday Edition," and "I Hate Christmas Main Character vs I Love Christmas Main Character." I need something better to put in the window, but I'm not quite sure what.

My grandma usually helps me with this too, but I'm afraid to even bring it up. She's keeping herself busy with our usual holiday traditions of decorating and cooking. But I'm worried she is getting depressed. She isn't coming into the store, she isn't reading—as far as I can tell—and she doesn't even want to talk about the pending eviction. It's starting to worry me, but I don't know what else I can do. Whenever I try to bring it up, she shoves food in my face and changes the subject. I know that's her way of saying *I'm okay,* but it doesn't make me feel any better.

On the way home, I have to stop in town and grab our Christmas tree so we can put it up and decorate tonight. We've only ever gotten real trees because Grandma says it's not a real Christmas without one. I love the smell of them and the way it makes the whole house feel like Christmas.

The last thing on my to-do list is to order the needed supplies for the fundraiser. It isn't a lot—mainly tablecloths and twinkle lights I can always repurpose for the store after the event. I head into the store and do the ordering at the register. I'm here alone, and I don't want to worry about missing any customers if I go in the back office, which proves to be right when I have to keep pausing what I'm doing to help people who walk in.

A little while after I've finished up ordering, I feel a gust of wind as the shop door opens.

"Good afternoon, Jax." Andrea smiles, walking in with a big winter coat.

"Hey, Andrea." I wave as I finish up with a customer.

Andrea shrugs off her coat and carries it to the back office. I follow her, and she's putting her name badge on her sweater. She's a few inches taller than I am, with a thin figure.

"Is it snowing yet?" I ask.

"Oh, yes, it's just starting, but it's supposed to get bad later," she says.

"If it's getting too bad and you need to close up, just shoot me a text and lock up. I don't want you getting stuck here."

"Are you sure?" she asks, surprised.

"Yes. Trust me. I can't guarantee the heat will work, and you might freeze. If it gets too bad, head home and let me know. Don't second-guess it," I tell her firmly.

"Okay, got it." She nods.

"I have to go grab a Christmas tree, but I'll see you tomorrow?"

"Yes. And I signed up to help with the fundraiser. I signed up my sisters, too. I don't know what we can do, but I figured more bodies can be helpful." She smiles.

"Thank you. I hope you know I'm doing everything I can to keep this place open."

"I know—don't stress. I'm good."

"Okay, have a good night."

Andrea follows me to the front of the store as I put my winter attire on. It's a bit of overkill, but I don't want to be cold, especially if it's already snowing. The man selling Christmas trees is someone I went to high school with. I can never remember his name, but we used to buy from his dad before he took over the family business. Before I got to work this morning, I picked out the one I wanted and asked him to keep it on hold for me. I don't want all the good ones to be gone by the time I get done with work.

The whole process is fairly fast and simple. The owner helps me load it onto the top of my car, and I head home.

Thankfully, the roads are okay; there's someone plowing already, so at least I can get home without any problems. The snow is falling, but just enough to make it annoying—not enough to stick. I park in the driveway and carry the tree in through the garage. I cut the netting off it, and the bristles fall all over the living room floor. I expect it, so I vacuum it up quickly and step back to look at it.

"You picked a good one; I can tell it has good bones," my grandma says with a smile. It takes a day or two for the branches to relax after being tied up all that time. But it's as big as we usually get.

"Thanks. I had them put it aside for me this morning."

"That's smart; who knows, after the storm we're getting, if they'll have any tomorrow." My grandma nods. She takes a seat on the recliner and pulls out her knitting.

"I told Andrea to head home if the snow gets too bad. I don't want her getting stuck at the store," I tell her.

"Smart. I made dinner—I wasn't sure when you'd be home, so I ate, but there are leftovers on the stove. Whatever you don't want, you can pack up."

"Couldn't find the lids to the containers again?" I tease. My grandma can't ever find the right lid for her containers. For whatever reason, it's like a puzzle she can't solve.

"I swear you change them up on me!" she exclaims.

"They all have matches when I go to do it." I laugh.

"Exactly! You know where the matches are hidden," she says playfully.

"No one is hiding Tupperware lids from you, I promise, Grandma." I kiss her head and chuckle to myself.

SEVEN

El

———

"You guys are on a break again?" Bells asks over FaceTime. I'm painting my toenails, so she's propped up on the edge of my bed as I open the red polish.

"Yeah. It just seems like the right idea since we're only fighting." I sigh.

"What are you fighting about?" she asks, raising an eyebrow.

"Nothing, but also everything?" I laugh anxiously.

"Explain?" She looks at me, confused.

I sigh. "It's like…I don't know. Have you ever just wanted to feel wanted? Like in every sense of the word—sexually, emotionally, physically?"

"Well, yeah. Honestly, that's how I feel about Tills," she says about her new girlfriend.

"I don't feel that with Tara. I feel like I have to ask for everything or tell her what I like or talk everything to death." I frown and lean to fix the toenail I just smudge.

"Have you ever felt that with someone?" Bells asks.

I pause, but the only person who comes to mind is Jax. For some reason, as much as we don't get along, I can still feel things with her. It's like this overwhelming passion or intensity that I just can't seem to shake. We've only been in the same room together once, but the tension was high. I just wanted to kiss her. Of course, I never would, but I also feel like, when she looks at me, she wants to take me against the nearby wall. Which I would never let her do, but a little fantasy? Why can't Tara be like that? Why is it so hard for her to just want me?

"I can tell by the look on your face that the answer to that is yes." Bells chuckles.

"Is it wrong that I just want someone to make me feel something?" I groan.

"No, but have you talked to Tara about it?"

"Yes, she knows that I'm looking for more affection, more time out of her busy schedule, and more nights where it's just the two of us. But I feel like a nag whenever I bring it up. She makes me feel like I'm asking for too much." I sigh.

It isn't the first time we've taken a break. At least once a year at this point, we take space, don't talk for a bit, and then decide to be together again. Maybe that's just how our relationship is? It isn't natural to want to spend every waking moment with someone, is it? Maybe I just need to accept that this is the kind of relationship we'll have.

"Maybe it's time to look at the facts—that you guys have run your course?" Bells says.

"I don't want to make any rash decisions, but I feel so complacent in every realm of my life. It's hard to feel excited about anything. Do you ever feel like that?"

"I used to feel that way before I inherited the orchard. I think I'm just supposed to be complacent in my job, feel whatever about love, and go through the motions of things. But being here completely changes my point of view. It's like, why am I living my life settling for things that don't make me immensely happy?" Bells says, smiling.

"That's what I want. I just don't know how to find that." I sigh.

"Well, when was the last time you felt overwhelming joy? Was it something you were doing or somewhere you were?" Bells asks, and I pause to think.

"I mean, besides getting drinks with you, it's spending time with my sister. Paige and I might disagree on things, but we had a nice weekend talking and spending time together," I admit.

"So start there. Maybe visiting her or having her visit you again wouldn't be the worst thing," Bells says.

"You're right." I nod.

Bells and I hang up, and I text Paige asking if she's free this weekend to come visit me in the city.

PAIGE: Sorry sis, I'm working and got stuff going on this weekend.

ME: No worries.

PAIGE: Why don't you come to me? I have time in between to see you 😊

ME: I don't know…

PAIGE: It's up to you.

PAIGE: But last time wasn't so bad right?

ME: Fine. I'm looking at train schedules.

PAIGE: YAY!!

I'm not exactly thrilled about going back to Evergreen Valley, but at least I don't have to see my parents. Hopefully I can sneak into town without them knowing and have a calm weekend with my sister. If she has too much going on, I can always come home early. But at least when she's free, we can chat and hang out. The next train is in fifteen minutes, but there's no way I'm making that. So I let my sister know I'll be on the one after that—in two hours. I start gathering my things and packing up for the weekend trip. It takes me a while to pack, and I decide to eat before I go so I don't have to buy food. I never eat anything from Grand Central—I've seen one too many roaches there, and I'm not taking the risk.

Heading to Grand Central, I take the six-train downtown. I

realize I didn't really think this through; it's a Friday afternoon, and Grand Central is as crowded as Times Square. It's hell because I'm sweating in my winter coat inside the subway, but I know the second I'm off it I'll be freezing again. Winters in New York City aren't for the weak. I'm bustling through crowds of tourists who are acting like the ceiling is the freaking Sistine Chapel. Sure, the zodiac paintings are cool, but it's not worth breaking your neck over to try and get a picture of. There are too many people coming into the city for date nights, people getting home from work, and tourists traveling. I should've thought ahead, but I'm already here, and it's too late to turn back now.

There's a couple kissing by the big clock in the center of Grand Central, and I almost push them out of the way so I can see the train departure schedule. They're too enveloped in each other to even see me. My train is on time, but there's no track number yet. That's something I despise about Grand Central—they won't put the track number up until the last minute, and then everyone has to make a run for it. There's no rhyme or reason to it, as far as I can tell, which sucks because I don't even know if my train is on this floor or not.

The Starbucks has a line out the door, which is disappointing. Unfortunately, the only smaller-owned coffee shop is on the other side of the building, and I don't have time for that. I glance at my Apple watch and head to the ticket booth to get a physical ticket. The app never works for me, and I don't want to pay more on board. Once I have my ticket, I hang out by one of the screens with the upcoming train departures, waiting for the track number to pop up.

Just as I predict, as they announce track 112, everyone makes a mad dash for it—myself included, knowing if I don't go now, I might not have a chance at a seat all the way up. I get to the gate for track 112 and race down the stairs, passing people who are walking way too slow for my liking. I'm one of the later stops on the train, so I make my way to the first car. It's also deemed the "quiet" car, so at least I don't have to worry about some asshole being on the phone the whole ride. That's happened one too many times. An old man huffs as I pass him without a second look—I'm not in the mood to wait for people to get a move on. The second I get to the first car, the train doors slide open, and I grab a seat, put my extra bag on the shelf above me, and relax a bit. Now all I have to do is hope no one wants to sit next to me.

There are no single seats on the Metro-North, and when it's full, like it will be tonight, I'm bound to have to sit next to someone. I just hope they aren't a yapper or someone eating something gross. One time, a man opened a container of street food from one of the vendors, and it was covered in onions. He spent the entire train ride eating as slow as possible. Everything smelled like onions. It was the equivalent to having a crying baby on a long flight.

I close my eyes, relaxing a bit as everyone else boards the train. I'm doing fine until an older man tries sitting next to me.

"This seat taken?" he asks, looking at the empty seat next to me.

"Nope." I shake my head.

"Could you move over then?" He looks at me, and I frown. I'm over as much as I can be—where the hell does he want me to go?

"Uh, no, sorry. My body is already against the window," I explain politely.

"Well, that's ridiculous!" He scoffs. He shakes his head so hard his glasses almost fall off his face.

"Excuse me?"

"I can't have a seat because your fat ass is taking up two of them!" he yells.

My eyes widen in surprise. "What the fuck?" is all I manage.

"Whatever." The old man takes off in another direction, and I stare at him in shock.

Surely, I didn't hear this guy correctly. Because what the actual fuck? I know I'm plus-sized—there's no hiding my body or my curves—but I don't take up two seats. I take up the one

I'm in, and maybe my ass is a little onto the other seat. What does he want me to do? Somehow shrink my ass?

The ride up is uneventful after that, but I'm pissed. Who the fuck does that guy think he is? Why do old people think they can just say things with no consequences? By the time I'm getting off in Evergreen Valley, I'm fuming. And of course, my sister is running late, so I have to walk from the train station to the nearby diner. It isn't too far, but I'm already exhausted and pissed off. So when I feel something hit me in the back of my coat, I turn around, fuming.

"WHAT THE HELL WAS THAT?!" I look around to find Jax and a group of kids who can't be older than ten, standing behind a snowman.

"Take it easy, Gomez." Jax chuckles.

She's wearing a dark coat, red gloves, and a red hat that covers most of her dark hair except for a few spare curls. Her cheeks are rosy like she's been out here a while, and she has a green scarf tied around her neck. There are snowflakes all over her, even though it isn't currently snowing.

"That isn't my name," I grumble. I'm not in the mood for this.

"I see someone hasn't read the book I gave them." She smirks. God, why does someone so annoying have to be so freaking hot?

"Some of us don't have time to read and build snowmen with children," I say angrily.

"We're also having a snowball fight." Jax laughs.

"You threw a snowball at me?" I ask, realizing that's what hit me in the back.

"Maybe?" Jax shrugs. "Maybe you got caught in the crossfire."

"Maybe if you spent more time at your business doing your job, you wouldn't have to worry about saving it," I say. I know it's a low blow, but it's worth it to see the angry reaction she has.

Jax picks up a handful of snow, and before I know what she's doing, she makes it into a ball and tosses it right toward me. She has a great arm, because it almost hits me in the face, but I duck at the last second. She laughs, as do all the kids around her, and it only pisses me off even more. How fucking old is she? Isn't this a little childish? Like, come on, doesn't she have better things to do all day than play in the snow?

"Better get going. I can't keep them from hitting any enemy of mine!" Jax shouts, and I realize all the kids are working on making snowballs to throw at me.

I have to run to the diner to keep myself safe. It isn't until I'm inside the warm building that I'm actually safe. I look out through the glass door—Jax is high-fiving each of the kids. I'm out of breath, and everyone in the diner is looking at me like a weirdo, but I don't care at this moment. What the hell is that? Has Jax really just sent a bunch of random kids to throw snow at me? I thought she was going to be an adult about this, but I guess not.

"Are you okay, dear?" an older woman with snow-white hair and a waitress apron asks.

"Yeah, thanks." I nod.

I don't need this town starting more rumors about me or my family. At this point I doubt anyone recognizes me, but if I say too much, I know my visit will get back to my dad. I take off my coat and wait quietly at the counter for my sister to get here. Ordering a simple cup of coffee I don't bother drinking, I leave a nice tip behind. I don't want anyone thinking I'm an asshole. But I'm also not about to drink some coffee I'm sure has been sitting around since this morning.

I can see Jax and the kids playing in the snow nearby. They pay me no attention as they run around, piling snowballs at Jax at one point. She's laughing and smiling ear to ear. I don't know who the kids are, but it's clear this is something she does often with them. They all feel comfortable with her, and she looks happy being with them.

Is it possible I've judged her too harshly? She only hates me because of my family. And maybe she didn't throw the snowball on purpose. Maybe she isn't as bad as I think. Not like I can go for her in the way I sometimes think about, but maybe I can be a little nicer. Hopefully I don't have to deal with her again—it'll be a moot point. This will be my last trip to Evergreen Valley.

EIGHT

Jax

"You're home late today," my grandma says, coming to the front door as I walk in. I shrug my jacket off outside, attempting to get off most of the snow.

"Snowball fight with the kids in town," I explain. I know she thinks I'm this big kid when I play with them, but I think it's fun. It's nice that they always ask me, and this community can use a hand to keep things on track.

"That's nice you went. I was worried you'd be too holed up at work." She wipes snow off my shoulders as I sit to take off my shoes.

"I knew it was coming, so I arranged for Andrea to take over," I explain.

"You really should let that poor girl find another job. It's not going to be fair when she doesn't have one at the end of the month." My grandma shakes her head.

"She knows I'm doing everything I can to keep the place open. Besides, we hired her for the winter—it's a seasonal position," I say.

"There may not be a place in a few weeks! You're wasting your time with this nonsense!" she says angrily.

"I know you think it's a waste of time, but Parker and I are making real strides. If everything goes according to plan, then we might be able to raise the funds."

"Yeah, and I might shit rainbows!" She throws her hands in the air and walks away angrily.

I get where she's coming from. This is a battle she's been fighting for far too long. But now it's a generational battle that I'm willing to take on and win. I follow her into the kitchen, where she's cooking pasta and eggplant parmigiana. It smells divine, and I'm starving. She's already eaten—the plate she's making is for me.

"I saw the daughter of the Monroes today. The kids and I tossed a snowball at her back." I snicker.

"Good, serves her right showing her face here again." My grandma cracks a smile.

"She walked right off the train and into our fight. She was so angry. It was so funny. She actually ran into the diner just to avoid us hitting her." I laugh.

"Oh yeah?"

"Yeah, the kids and I were hoping she'd leave while we were still there—so we could attack again—but we never saw her again." I frown.

My grandma gives me a weird look.

"What?" I ask.

"You're talking an awful lot about someone you claim to hate." She gives me a knowing look, and I clench my fist around the fork.

"She's terrible. I only bring her up because she was at the fight," I lie. I can't tell my grandma how I never stop thinking about her.

"Mmm-hmm." I know she knows I'm lying, so I don't push it further.

I hate that I think about Eliora. I hate that she looks so good in her black peacoat that hugs each curve of hers. I hate that I love the way her cheeks get red when she's angry. And I especially hate the fact that I think about her when she clearly doesn't think about me. I mean, I bet she hasn't even read the book I gave her. She's just as stuck-up and money hungry as the rest of her family. The only one of the Monroes who seems to be somewhat normal is Paige. I called her boss and confirmed using the rec room, even ensuring Paige isn't in charge of the room so she won't be able to take it away or ruin the event in any way. Maybe Paige is adopted, because there's no way she's related to the rest of them.

"Why don't you come watch a movie with me? *It's a Wonderful Life* is on." She smiles.

"It's on because you probably put it in the DVD player. I don't think you know how to work Netflix," I tease. I put my empty plate in the sink, rinse off the leftover sauce residue, and place it in the dishwasher.

"So? It's still on." She makes a face at me, and I laugh. Sometimes she's like the kids I play with.

"Fine, but I have to finish putting up the lights while I watch. It's been driving me crazy all day," I admit. I start putting them up last night but got too tired and had to call it a night.

"Whatever you want." She shrugs and sits on her recliner in the living room.

Grandma turns on the movie, and the opening scenes of *It's a Wonderful Life* appear on the screen. We prefer the black-and-white version to the color one—it feels more authentic. I grab the stepladder from the closet and start stringing the lights where I left off on the side of the living room. My grandma and I love a house full of Christmas lights for the whole season. The tree is full of them, decorated beautifully with fifty years' worth of ornaments. The rest of the house needs to match the tree, hence why there are so many lights.

There's tinsel and cute signs and decorative pillows all over the house. The only place we don't have decorations is in the front yard. It doesn't make sense to have much besides a festive holiday sign on our front door. We don't have neighbors who go caroling, and there aren't any kids on our corner of the town.

Plus, my grandma is convinced if I don't put them up right, they might blow away with the winter winds.

"I don't get how you love this movie," my grandma comments, looking at her knitting. She knows I can hear her. She's never liked this movie, and I've always loved it.

"It's a nice Christmas story," I tell her.

"The man commits suicide and hallucinates a ghost only to realize it's not true. Most of the movie isn't even set at Christmastime," she grumbles.

"But it's a nice story about how much a person touches others' lives without even knowing it," I say. I swear we have the same argument every year.

"Mmm." She shakes her head. She pretends to be more focused on her knitting so she doesn't have to reply, which is usually a sign that I've won the argument.

NINE

El

"**Y**ou're going where?!" I squeal when Paige finishes talking.

"I'm going to help Jax and her friends paint decorations for the gala they're having." Paige shrugs.

"The gala they're having to raise money so our family won't get the bookstore?" I ask, clarifying. Has she completely lost her mind?

"Yes." She nods, pulling on an old pair of sweatpants.

"Paige, you're joking, right? If Dad finds out, he's going to lose it." I look at her, waiting for some semblance of realization that doesn't come.

"They're painting at the library because we have the extra-huge rec room attached to the back. And that's where they're hosting the event," she explains.

"You got your job to host their event?!" I look at her, exasperated.

"Yes. It was my idea," she says, and I throw my arms in the air in defeat.

"Paige, please tell me this is all some sort of elaborate plan."

"Nope. I told you I don't agree with what you and Dad are

doing, so I'm going to help them get things on track," she says, smiling.

"I see," I say, even though I don't. I don't know what else I can possibly say at this point.

"Why don't you come with me?" she says.

"What?" I look at her like she has three heads, or maybe she's smoking something.

"What? It's open to the community, and they need all the help they can get." She shrugs.

"Wouldn't that be like..." I don't know the right word for it.

"Jax is cool. I'm sure if you show up it won't be a big deal." Paige smiles.

For a moment I wonder if there's something going on with Paige and Jax. Paige is bisexual, and as far as I know, she isn't seeing anyone. I know I don't have a leg to stand on, but for some reason that makes me jealous. I guess I'm coming along, just to see if there's something going on there.

"Fine, I'll go." I sigh in defeat.

"Great! But change into something you don't care about. We'll be painting, and I can't promise you won't get messy," she says, looking me over.

"Okay," I grumble.

I don't have too many options, but I brought a pair of leggings and a T-shirt from college to use as pajamas. I'll have to settle and use those as painting clothes. Not that I'm very artistic, but I guess I'll have to do what I can to blend in.

The library is right in town, literally right next door to our father's office buildings. But it's unlikely he's working on a Sunday afternoon. We head inside, right for the rec room, something I haven't seen since I was a kid. Unlike my sister, I don't spend a lot of time around the library. I'm shocked to see how many people are here to help Jax. Paige disappears on me, going to talk to someone while I stand around awkwardly. A few minutes later, she returns with Jax and a bigger smile.

"Jax, you remember my older sister, El? She's here to help out today," Paige introduces us.

"You're here to help?" Jax raises an eyebrow at me. Of course she doesn't trust me—I don't blame her. And frankly I'm not one hundred percent sure why I'm here anyway.

"Yes." I grit my teeth. "I'm sorry, I left my gloves at home, so no snowball fights today." I glare.

"Too bad. I'm sure the kids would love another chance. I know I would." She smirks.

"Am I missing something?" Paige asks, looking between us, confused.

"Nope, just here to help. Put me to work," I say.

"Fine, you can be in charge of washing brushes. I don't see how you could mess that up too badly," Jax says sassily.

"Sounds good. Point me to the sink." I smile. I'm not going to let her get to me.

Jax walks me to the slop sink in the back of the rec room, and it's already filled with dirty paintbrushes. How many freaking paintbrushes do they have? And how many do they need washed?

"Hope this will be up to your standards, Gomez." She smirks.

"You know I still have no idea what that means." I roll my eyes.

"I know, which only makes it funnier." She chuckles to herself before leaving me in here alone.

I roll up my sleeves, tie up my curls into a messy bun, and get to work. The brushes are mainly simple to clean except for a few that have the paint caked on them. But every time I'm finished, Jax just brings me more and takes the clean ones. I don't even know what they're painting. So much for being able to scope out if Jax and Paige are a thing.

After a few hours of this pattern, I get a break and use it to do some stalking. I don't know much about Jax, and it seems like a rookie move. Isn't the old saying, keep your friends close and your enemies closer? Not that I'm convinced Jax is the enemy. But doing a little more research never hurts. I go to Instagram first, but it's surprisingly tame—just photos of her with books and selfies with who I assume is her grandmother.

It links me to the bookstore's Instagram, which is actually pretty successful. They have over 10,000 followers, which isn't a ton, but it's more than I think they'd have. The posts are mainly about new books, and they aren't exactly the most aesthetic, but I guess it works for them. Although the latest post is from months ago. I scroll back as much as I can until I notice that it says "one of the first romance-only bookstores in the US." Is that true?

I do a little googling and come up with a handful of articles that show it's true. Apparently, they were one of the first, and that was almost fifty years ago. Most of the articles say the same thing—that no one thought it will be this successful. They believe a bookstore with only one genre is a recipe for disaster. Of course, none of these articles happen to mention now how long this place has been open. Consider me impressed.

I think if the place is advertised and marketed a little better it might not have to be doing this gala. If they put effort into TikTok or really any social media, I'm sure they could get things going. I wonder why Jax never thought of that? If the place is hemorrhaging money, shouldn't they be exploring every avenue?

"You have time to be on your phone? I thought you were here to help," Jax says, shaking my focus. I slip my phone into my pocket.

"I'm done—just taking a break." I shrug.

"Of course you are. You could've come to take the new brushes yourself, but instead you're checking what? TikTok?" Jax scoffs.

"Hey, I'm here as a volunteer. I don't have to be here," I remind her.

"Then why are you here?" She glares at me.

"I'm here as a favor to my sister. She seems to think it's important, and apparently you need all the help you can get," I tease.

"And whose fault is that?" Jax clenches her sharp jaw.

"Uh, yours for not paying your mortgage?" Is she really trying to insinuate this is my fault?

"It isn't like you or your family couldn't offer us a bit of leeway with that, right? But no! You've been after my grandma's property for years, and now you have us right where you want us!" Jax yells.

"Why is it our family's job to fix your family's mistakes?!" I say angrily.

"Whoa! What's going on here?" an unfamiliar redhead asks, cracking open the door.

"Nothing," I say angrily.

"Of course you'd say that." Jax scoffs under her breath.

"I'm just saying—we can hear you all the way out there," the redhead says softly.

"Great." Jax sighs and storms out.

"I'm Parker, by the way…" the redhead says, looking at me with a cocked head.

"El," I offer.

"Oh," Parker says knowingly. "The Monroes' daughter."

"Yup." Great, I'm infamous. Or maybe that means Jax talks about me? It probably isn't the latter.

I turn my back to Parker, washing the rest of the brushes. I don't want to be here, but I'm not going to prove her right by leaving. And she does need the help. I get some of my frustration out on the brushes, scrubbing extra hard to get the tough paint off. No one comes to visit me, and the next batch of brushes comes from Parker instead of Jax.

"Did you really get into a screaming match with Jax?" Paige asks, popping up behind me.

"She started it." I roll my eyes.

Paige sighs. "Can you blame her? I'm trying to get her to trust me, and you do this?"

"Why do you want her to trust you anyway?" I scoff.

"Because she lives in this town, El, and if you haven't noticed, the queer community is small enough. I don't need to alienate half of it because of our last name." She sighs.

"Do you have a thing for her?" I ask, since she opened the door to this.

"No. I'm sort of seeing this guy," she says casually.

"Oh."

"It's nothing serious, but we're enjoying each other for now," she says with a shrug.

"I'm just happy if you're happy."

"Then it would make me happy if you got along with Jax," she says, looking at me knowingly.

"Fine, I'll do my best." I frown.

"Thank you. Now come join us. I think we can manage without some of the brushes." She pulls me out of the washroom to where everyone is painting.

"Is your boyfriend here?" I ask quietly, looking around the room.

"Don't call him that!" she whispers back. "But no, he's at work."

"That's good. A man with a job is good."

"God, you're so gay you don't even know how to be happy about a man." Paige laughs.

"I'm sorry—I'm trying." I laugh back. Jax glares at me from across the room, but I try to ignore her, for Paige's sake.

Quietly, I help Paige paint the background of a few different things. I don't know exactly what we're making, but I get the feeling Paige and I are being put on tasks no one cares about. That way, if we mess them up, it won't be the end of the world. They don't trust us because of our last name—because of our attachment to our family. It's something I'm used to, but I've never noticed it so blatantly. Especially not directed at my sister.

I'm protective of her, even though she has never needed it before.

When we're done for the day, Paige drives us home, and her roommates greet us with cocktails and the smell of cookies.

"It's a crantini—cranberry juice and gin," her roommate, Elliott, says, handing me the glass. They have this gorgeous dark brown hair they keep in a ponytail and wear glasses that perfectly show off their dark eyes.

I take a sip and am surprised at how good it is. "I'm not usually a gin fan, but this is good."

"Did you bring home the tinsel and marshmallows?" Paige's other roommate, Sierra, asks Paige. She's Paige's age with short blonde hair and a variety of tattoos. I've been here several times, and every time I see her, I notice a new tattoo.

Paige groans. "Oh shit. I knew I was forgetting something." She looks at me. "Are you good here? I'll be back in like twenty minutes—I just have to run to the store."

"Yeah, I'm okay." I nod.

"Okay, anything else for anyone?" Paige asks around.

"Can you get more cranberry juice? We have plenty of liquor, but I forget to grab juice," Elliott says, pouring out the last of the juice into his glass.

"Juice, marshmallows, and tinsel—got it." Paige nods and grabs her car keys.

"So, El, right? Paige says you live in the city? How do you like it?" Elliott asks. They're putting ornaments on a Christmas tree as I sit on the couch with my drink.

"I love it, honestly. I'm definitely a New York City transplant for life," I joke.

"I grew up on the Upper West Side. Sometimes I think about going back, but it moves so fast," Sierra says.

"That's what I like about it," I laugh. "Growing up here, it's so intimidating—everyone knows everything about you. In the city, I can be myself, and no one bats an eye."

"Isn't that sort of lonely, though?" Elliott frowns.

"It can be, but I don't personally think it is." I sip my drink.

"The cookies are ready!" Paige's last roommate, Regina, calls from the kitchen.

We all jump up and head to the kitchen. Regina is pulling a second tray of cookies from the oven and placing each one on a cooling rack. There's already a batch waiting on a Christmas plate for us. These cookies are brown but shaped like snowflakes, so I assume them to be gingerbread flavored. I've never seen gingerbread cookies that aren't shaped like people, but they're delicious. Regina has dark skin with tight braided hair and an athletic body. I think she's closer to my age than Paige's, but she's still in school, finishing her master's degree.

"Dude, these are awesome," Elliott says, stuffing their mouth full of cookies.

"Save some for Paige. If she comes back and there are none left, she'll kill you," Regina scolds him.

"Fine." Elliott takes another when Regina turns her back, making Sierra and me laugh.

"Elliott!" Regina yells.

"Come on! You guys are the worst!" He puts the cookie back and stalks back to the living room.

"I'm back!" Paige announces and carries the grocery bags into the kitchen. "El, grab the tinsel, and we'll start with the tree."

"Okay." I take the tinsel out of the package, and she grabs a few cookies before heading to the living room with me. She steals a sip of my drink as I wait for her to tell me what to do next.

"Elliott, where's the Christmas music? I was promised a playlist," Paige complains.

"Oh crap! I'm on it!" They scramble for their phone and set up the speaker to start blasting Mariah Carey's "All I Want for Christmas Is You."

"That's more like it," Paige smiles, and I laugh. Too many times have we sung this song badly in our rooms as we decorate for the holidays. "Come on, toss the tinsel anywhere. This tree looks naked."

I throw a bit on the side of the tree, and then I grab a handful and pour it on my sister's head. She laughs, grabs more, and tosses it at me. It turns into a tinsel war that all of her roommates join in for. We're a little tipsy, tinsel everywhere, and we can't stop laughing.

TEN

Jax

"Paige brought her sister again?" I scoff when I see them walk in together.

"Maybe she's here to help?" Parker says.

"Because she was such a big help last time?"

"It's not like you let her do much more than wash brushes. She did help enough with that," Parker says quietly.

"It's not my fault I can't trust them. Our families have been feuding for years; that can't be erased overnight." I sigh.

"I know, I'm just saying maybe you should give them both a chance. I'm sure they personally weren't the ones behind the eviction," Parker says.

"El is a lawyer; you don't think she has anything to do with it?" I scoff.

"How do you know she's a lawyer? Did you look into her?" Parker smirks.

"Maybe I did; I want to know what I'm getting myself into. It's important to not have any more surprises," I say.

"Mm," Parker hums, smirking.

"What?" I frown.

"I've seen the way you look at her; I don't think you hate her as much as you claim to."

"As if." I roll my eyes. I don't think it's that obvious. I try keeping my attraction to her a secret, but it doesn't help when Paige keeps parading her sister around. This is the second weekend in a row they're both here helping out.

"Hey, where should we jump in?" Paige asks, coming over to Parker and me. El is trailing quietly behind her.

"You're late." I cross my arms and look past Paige to El.

"That's my fault; my train was late. I'm sorry," El says.

"Of course it was," I mumble.

"You can join in with any group that needs help. We're just putting together the baskets for the silent auction. We want them to look as beautiful as they can so they get higher bids," Parker explains.

"Sounds good." Paige smiles, and El gives me a look, but she doesn't say anything.

"Can't you be nice?" Parker pokes me in the arm when they're out of earshot.

"I probably could be," I tease. Parker glares at me, so I sigh. "Fine, yes, I can be."

"Good, it might help if both of Mr. Monroe's daughters are on your side. Maybe, if we can't raise the funds, they can convince him to take back the eviction," Parker says.

"You don't think we'll raise the funds?" That's the only thing I hear from what she says.

"No, I do. I'm just saying it doesn't hurt to have them on our side."

I nod. I can't go down that path of thinking. I need this place to stay open. It's my entire life, mine and my grandma's. She's finally come back to the store, but only after my many, many pleas. She isn't here today, which is why I have Andrea manning the register while we use the office and a bit of the store to create baskets. The library has an event going on, so we can't use the rec room, and this is the best we can do. During the week, all the local businesses dropped off items for baskets. Parker, Shiloh, and I went thrifting and found cheap baskets of different sizes to put the items in.

The bakery is the only place that hasn't donated anything yet. They want to donate fresh items, and with the event a few weeks away, we obviously can't take anything yet. The diner donated some merch with their logo; the toy store donated some popular kids' toys as well as a gift card; and the local bar donated some beer glasses with their logo, along with a T-shirt. There's more around here, but this is just the beginning. Everyone is really coming together the way Parker and I had hoped. I'm nervous, but it's obvious Mr. Monroe has rubbed everyone the wrong way. Everyone wants a chance to help in any way they can—because they all know they could be next.

El is across the room. I know I shouldn't worry about what she's doing, but I can't help it. I don't trust her, and I know she's up to no good. It isn't like there's a lot for her to mess up, but I don't want to give her the chance either. I take inventory of what Paige is doing too, but she's cutting the plastic wrap for the baskets perfectly. She's talking to the other volunteers and looks like she actually belongs here. When I glance back at El, I see her working on the basket for the bar. She's holding one of the beer cups, inspecting it. I'm not sure what she's looking for, but she holds it up a little high, and before I know it, it slips from her grip and shatters into a million pieces all over the hardwood floor. The place goes silent as everyone turns to see what happened. I slam down the scissors I'm using as Parker rushes to get a broom. I knew I couldn't trust her to do anything.

"Are you kidding me?" I say angrily to El. She stands from the stool she's sitting in.

"I'm okay; it slipped, but I didn't get cut," El says, like that's something I'm worried about.

"You're joking, right?"

"It was an accident… I didn't mean to," El says. Surely, she's joking.

"I'm sure it wasn't," I say sarcastically. "But now we have an incomplete basket and no way to replace it. I can't ask Teddy's to replace it; I'm not trying to steal from another local business," I say angrily. Parker starts sweeping up the glass behind us.

"I can pay to replace it," El offers.

"Of course, you can—when don't the Monroes throw money at their problems?" I scoff.

"What the hell is your problem? I know I broke a glass, but I don't think it's as serious as you're making it out to be," El says, her tone sharper than before.

"You're joking, right? We're here because of you and your family. We have to scrounge for cash and raise money making these baskets because of your family. So you breaking one of them kind of pisses me off." I step closer to her, and her breath hitches. I glare into her dark brown eyes.

"Jax, maybe just take a moment to cool off," Parker says quietly, putting a hand on my shoulder.

"I'm fine."

"You should listen to your friend; I don't think you're in a position to lose anything else," El says with a smirk.

"What the hell is that supposed to mean?" I clench my fists at my side.

"It's clear you're not going to make enough with a few baskets and some party. I don't know why you don't just give up now," El says, crossing her arms over her chest.

"El…" Paige starts, but we ignore her.

"No. You clearly think you know better; then what are you even doing here?" I say.

"Come with me." Parker grabs my hand unexpectedly and starts walking me somewhere. I can count on my hand the number of times we've held hands, and all of them I was drunk and she was leading me somewhere. So Parker holding my hand is severely out of character for us. Just as I'm about to question where, she grabs Eliora's hand too. It's clear she's bringing us somewhere, but for God knows what. She drags us both to the back office and then to the back supply closet. What are we doing in here?

"What the hell?" Eliora and I say at the same time.

"You're going to stay in there until you can agree on something. You're both too hyped, and we can't get anything done until you can calm down," Parker says firmly.

"But what—" Parker ignores our desperate plea, and we stand there not facing the other, unsure of what just happened.

"We're in here because of you, you know," El says.

"Excuse me?!" I snap my head at her, and she only smiles.

"You heard me. You couldn't keep things professional; it's no wonder you can't keep a business running." She shrugs smugly.

"You need to stop saying shit you know nothing about," I grumble.

"Or what?" She steps closer, which is right in my airspace. It isn't like there's a ton of room in the supply closet. But now I can smell her lavender perfume, and it's intoxicating.

Without thinking about it, I pull her body into mine and kiss her. We've been dancing around this for weeks now, and I'm sick of it. I'm so attracted to her it's ridiculous, and I'm dying for a taste. I just need to know how it feels to kiss her; then maybe I can get it out of my head.

For a second she hesitates, but then her hands are in my hair, and she groans into my mouth. Fuck, why the hell does she have to kiss like this? My hands hold her body tightly against mine. Hers grip my curls like there's no tomorrow, and I slip my tongue in her mouth. She's so soft, her lips sweet like cherries, and I moan. Our bodies are fighting for friction against the other. All of our anger from the last few weeks is escaping as tension in this moment.

"Holy shit," she says breathlessly as she pulls away.

"Same." I don't know what to say. Is that just a fluke?

I'm about to ask when she kisses me again. This time not as hard as the first, but her lips melt into mine. Has this been what I need all along? I can't think about anything else in this moment.

El feels like nothing I've ever experienced. Her body is all curves, her belly bumping into mine. Her breasts are bigger than my head, and all I want is to stick my face between them. I also don't want to rush and expect too much from this.

El puts her hands on my chest and then pulls back from kissing. "Is this okay?"

"Hell yeah." I pull her into me, and I can feel her smile against my lips.

She bites down on my bottom lip, and I whimper. I fucking whimper for her. Who the hell am I? It's like she brings out this different side of me. She grabs the side of my boob and slides her hand around to grip it fully. My nipples harden under her touch, and I wish this didn't feel like a power struggle. I'm ready to fuck her right here; I'm embarrassingly wet. It has been too long since I've gotten laid, and the evidence of that is in my underwear.

El is rough with her movements, but none of them hurt. Each one is fueled with desire and passion that we've spent building. All the times we fought seem to disappear when her lips are on mine. A shiver runs down my spine as her fingertips brush gently against the side of my neck. She runs them all the way to my ear and holds my face in her hands. My tongue twists against hers, and she moans quietly with me. I pull back and grip the back of her neck with my hand. Tilting her head to the side, I bite down gently on her neck. Something about this makes me feel feral. She stops me just as I start to suck on her neck.

"Hey! No hickies! We're not teenagers!" she scolds me, and I laugh.

El rolls her eyes at me, and I go back to kissing her neck. I'm sliding my hands under her soft sweater to feel her chest. I grab her breasts through what feels like a lace bra. Her nipples are so hard I can feel them through the thick fabric. El moans lightly into my ear, and I kiss her. My lips tease hers as she aches for more that I won't give her. I like being in control in this moment.

I'll probably give it all up in a moment but knowing she wants me and can't have it thrills a new side of me.

I slip one hand in her bra and tug on her nipple. Immediately her head falls back, and she whimpers out a moan for me. I put my other hand on her mouth and look into her dark orbs. "You have to be quiet," I remind her.

"Mmm." She hums against my hand. I tug on her nipple again, and this time she bites my palm. I smirk, watching her reactions as I play with her breasts. They're so big and soft—like two pillows I want to lay my head onto.

El licks my palm, and I pull back, wiping my hand on my jeans. "What the hell?"

But El doesn't answer, instead pushing me back into the wall. Her hands are back on my chest, my breathing getting heavier with every touch. I'm anticipating more, trying not to get my expectations up, but also embarrassingly turned on. She unbuttons the first three buttons of my shirt, and I tense as her cool fingers brush against the tops of my breasts. She looks at me for confirmation before her hand explores my bra, finding my taut nipples begging to be touched.

I bite down on my bottom lip, careful not to be as loud as she was. She kisses my neck, her teeth scraping against the side of it. I clench the fabric of her sweater in my fists tightly. Why does neck kissing feel so godly yet make me want to do ungodly things? Her lips are soft; I can feel them against the goosebumps on my skin.

"Are you two okay? It's quiet and I—" Parker squeals as she opens the door and sees me, shirt unbuttoned, with El's hands on my chest. She just as quickly slams the door behind her. I turn red, thinking about my best friend catching us in the act.

El and I look at each other in panic, as if Parker opening the door is the cold shower we both desperately need. We change moods entirely. Holy fuck, what the hell do we just do? El and I jump apart, as far as we can for being in a supply closet. I fix my bra and rebutton my shirt. She fixes her hair and sweater, both of which are in disarray from our makeout. I try to think of what to say, but I'm not sure what this even is. I'm also not sure what I want. I know I don't want to be dating the enemy, but it's not like kissing means dating. Maybe it's just a hookup between… enemies?

"We should—" I start, but El is opening the door and running out of the building before I can say another word.

ELEVEN

El
—

Parker and I avoid eye contact as I race out of the supply closet and head for the front door. Paige gives me a weird look, but I ignore her too as I grab my jacket and go outside. The snow is fresh, only sticking from this morning, and squishes under my feet. I don't know where I'm going—it's not like I can leave Paige here alone. Nor can I exactly drive myself back to Paige's apartment. I decide to walk around the side of the bookstore and just burn some of this energy off. How could I kiss Jax? How could she kiss me?

My hands are shaking, thinking about how good it felt to be touched and kissed by her. I can't recall the last time it felt that good to be close to someone. I haven't kissed Tara in months, and the last time we did, it was more out of routine than a primal want. Jax feels like she lights a fire inside me I'm still buzzing from. The feeling is both intoxicating and terrifying.

"Are you okay? You sort of run away," Paige says, panting. She's out of breath from chasing after me.

"I'm fine," I lie.

"Did something happen? All Parker says is you and Jax were going to talk things out. But then you both came out still upset, and Parker looked like she saw a ghost," Paige explains.

"We're fine. We didn't talk anything out." I don't tell her about the kiss. I have no idea what it means, and I don't want to talk about it yet.

"Okay, are you coming back in? Or do you want me to take you home?" Paige rubs her hands together, breathing her warm air on them. She didn't grab her coat before coming after me.

"I'm fine. I need a few minutes alone, and I'll come back in," I reassure her. "But you go back in—you're going to get hypothermia."

"Fine, only because it's literally freezing out here." She nods and runs back inside.

I can still feel Jax's lips on mine, and I brush my fingers across them. It's like her lips are a ghost still there or something. I'm so freaking turned on, and we barely did anything. Why does she have to be so fucking hot? She and I are supposed to be enemies. We fight every time we see each other—where the hell did this come from? I thought she was interested in Paige, not me. Clearly, I was wrong.

"Meow."

I look around, confused. Did I just hear a meow? All around me is covered in white; there's nothing remotely looking like a cat. Maybe I'm hearing things now—at least that would explain why I kissed Jax. Well, let her kiss me.

"Meow."

There it is again. I walk around the side of the bookstore, trying to see if I can get closer to the sound. It's close but muffled. I step toward the front door, and it gets quieter, so I step back and go in the other direction. The meows get louder, and I bend lower to the ground. Maybe it's somewhere in the snow? It doesn't sound like it's hurt, but maybe it's stuck somewhere? I stop when I see the snow moving in one spot near the side of a tree.

Bending to my knees, I move some of the snow away softly, and a pair of dark eyes look back at me. The cat that is meowing at me has pure white fur. I keep moving the snow off the cat, who looks terrified of me.

"Hey, it's okay. I'm here to help you. I'm going to move the snow, and then I can see what's wrong," I tell the cat in a soothing tone. It seems like the cat is stuck or something, but I can't tell on what.

I move the snow off them, and then I see they have some kind of small plant stuck in their paw. Part of it is hanging out, while the rest of it is embedded in its paw. It looks at me and meows sadly. Shit, what can I do? I don't know if it's like with people—where you don't pull out the embedded item...or it's safe to pull it out.

"I'll be right back," I say.

I head back inside, and Jax is the first person I see. She looks like she wants to talk to me, so I start the conversation before she can mention the kiss.

"I need a box and a blanket or a coat or something," I tell her.

"What?" She looks at me with furrowed brows.

"There's a hurt cat outside, and I need a box to put it in, and maybe a blanket or something to keep it warm," I explain. "Quickly, because I don't want it to suddenly run away."

"Shit, okay. Hold on." Jax springs into action and grabs a large box and a white sheet from the office. She follows me outside with Paige, and I lead them to where the cat is.

"Are they okay?" Paige asks.

"They have something in their paw, but I don't know what to do. I think we should bring the poor thing to a vet," I explain.

"Doesn't Bells have a vet on her orchard? I feel like you told me that," Paige says.

"She does! Great idea!" I pull out my phone as Jax kneels in the snow to try to pick up the cat.

"Who's Bells?" Jax asks, but neither of us answers her. I'm too busy waiting for Bells to pick up.

"El?" Bells answers the phone.

"Hey! Do you have a vet on staff at the orchard?"

"Uh, yes. Did you adopt a pet or something?" Bells chuckles.

"I found a cat outside in the snow, and it's shivering and has something stuck in its paw. I'm hoping we can bring it to you and have the vet take a look," I explain.

"Yeah, Hattie is actually right next to me. Are you in the city? How are you bringing a cat on the train?" Bells asks.

"Actually, I'm in Evergreen."

"Oh, in that case, I think it's only an hour from here. I'll text you the details. Do you need to ask Hattie anything?" Bells asks.

"Yeah, do we leave the plant in their paw or take it out?" I ask. Bells repeats it to Hattie; I can hear mumbling, but the answer is too quiet.

"Hattie says leave it in; she'll take a look," Bells says.

"Okay! Thank you so much," I say, relieved. "Okay, we don't pull anything out, but we can bring her to Bells's orchard. They have a vet on staff who can help."

"Crap, I just realize I have to be home in an hour to make sure the heating guy delivers the oil for our furnace. I don't think we'd make it back in time if we go now," Paige frowns, looking at the time.

"You can't have them come later?" I ask.

"No, we're low, and if we skip it, they might not come for another week. It's a pain in the ass," Paige sighs.

"I can take you," Jax says quietly. She manages to pick up the cat and wrap her in the white sheet, keeping her front paw exposed—I assume to keep the plant from going in any deeper.

"Really?" I ask.

"Yeah, I don't want her in pain any longer. I'll talk to Parker about closing up, and we can go." Jax puts the cat in the box on the ground and heads inside.

"Wow, that was super nice." Paige looks at me skeptically.

"I know…" I pretend to be just as confused. I don't want to give any indication I know what that is about.

"Please don't kill each other in the car," Paige says sternly.

"I promise."

Pretending to be distracted by the cat, I bend down to let her sniff me before I pet her. She obliges, and I carefully pet her head while she meows. Jax is back a few minutes later in her coat, holding car keys. She lifts the box the cat is in effortlessly and leads us to her car.

"I'm going to put her in the back. I don't think she can jump around, but just in case," Jax explains. She puts the seat belt around the box for extra security.

"Do you have the address?" Jax looks at me, and I nod. Pulling out my phone, I rattle off the address Bells gave me.

"Your friend works at Sapphire Falls Orchard?" Jax says, impressed.

"Uh, she owns it now, actually."

"Oh, wow. I've been there a few times—it's a cute place," Jax says.

"I'll text you later to come pick you up—just let me know when," Paige says to me.

"I can bring her home—no sense making you come out again," Jax offers.

"Oh, that's so nice. Is that okay?" Paige asks me hesitantly.

"Uh, yeah, sure." I nod.

"Okay, see you later." Paige heads back for the bookstore, and I climb into Jax's passenger seat.

The first thing I notice is how ridiculously clean the car is. I mean, there's not a speck of dirt or a crumb anywhere. But the second thing I notice is how good it smells. It's Jax's usual scent of pine mixed with peppermint. It's like she's a walking Christmas candle. I'm going to have to spend the next hour smelling her? Fuck me now. I already know what she tastes like, and this is torture.

"So we should probably…" I start, but Jax cuts me off.

"It's fine. We don't have to talk about it," she says sharply.

"I mean, it's just…"

"It's really fine. It's a heat-of-the-moment mistake. It's not like it meant anything," she adds.

My heart sinks in my chest. "Right, of course."

"That would be crazy. The two of us? We fight like cats and dogs; it's not like it could be anything," she goes on.

"Got it," I say defensively.

I guess I'm the idiot who thinks the kiss was more than it is. Maybe Jax often makes out with women in supply closets, and this is just a normal day for her. Would it have kept going if we weren't interrupted? I don't want to think about that right now. God only knows who else she might hook up with in that closet. Here I am thinking I'm going to have to let her down gently, and she is the one surprising me. Whatever. I can have random makeouts and have it not mean anything. I won't let it bother me.

We're silent for the rest of the ride. I think it's safer that way —otherwise we'd probably just argue. The cat meows in the back, keeping it from being completely silent. When we pull up to the orchard, I call Bells to let her know we've arrived. She has us drive straight to the vet's house. Apparently, she has a small office in her home, and it's easier with the snow, although they don't have as much as we do. It isn't my first time visiting the orchard, but it's the first time in the winter, and things are a little different.

"Hey! I'm so happy to see you." Bells wraps her arms around me. "I wish it was for better reasons, but Hattie is the best. She'll be able to fix them right up."

"Awesome. I feel bad. I don't know how long they were out there. I just happened to stumble upon them," I explain.

"Come in. I'm Bells, and you are?" Bells ushers us in and introduces herself to Jax.

"Oh, sorry. This is Jax."

Bells's face lights up, looking between us, and I want to punch my best friend for being so obvious. Of course I indulged in telling her about my tiny crush, but it's not like I thought I'd ever act on it. Yet she was convinced otherwise. Jax notices

Bells's look and glances at me with a smirk. Great, I'll never be allowed to live this down.

"Jax—but I guess you've heard of me." Jax winks.

"Yeah, that you're an obnoxious flirt." I scoff.

"I don't flirt with you." Jax smirks, and I grumble.

"Hey, I'm Hattie—or Dr. Miller. You can bring the cat in here, and I'll take a look," Hattie says. She's a dark brunette with a nose ring and tons of tattoos. She doesn't look like any doctor I've ever met, but I'm not in a place to judge.

Jax carries the cat into her office, and Bells pulls me aside to gasp. "How could you not tell me how hot she is?! And why didn't you tell me you were bringing her?"

"You're joking, right? I was with her the entire car ride—I was afraid to tell you and have her see my texts," I whisper.

"I don't know why you two are feuding—she is hot as fuck," Bells says, admiring her.

"Who's hot?" Bells's girlfriend, Tilly, asks, stepping into the room. "Hey, El, nice to see you again." She gives me a one-armed hug and then looks at her girlfriend.

"I'm not saying for me, but for El? Jax is hot," Bells says quietly.

"Mmm, nice save, babe." Tilly chuckles.

"She's hot, but that doesn't make her anything," I shake my head.

Bells is about to complain when Hattie and Jax come back into the room.

"So the cat is okay. She doesn't have hypothermia, so she mustn't have been outside too long when you found her. I gave her a round of antibiotics to keep away any infection, just in case. Her paw should be okay in a few days. There was a piece of mistletoe stuffed in it," Hattie explains.

"Mistletoe?" Jax and I ask at the same time.

"Yeah, I guess she somehow got ahold of it. The actual plant can be a bit rough. It's rare that it hurts anyone, but it's sharp enough, and she clearly wasn't paying attention. I'm glad you brought her in, you'll need to keep an eye on her tonight for any residual symptoms. If she has any of them, bring her back or to the nearest vet hospital immediately. She'll be good as new in no time. Does she belong to someone?" Hattie asks and hands us a paper with mistletoe poisoning symptoms.

"Uh, we actually don't know. We just found her and brought her here," Jax explains.

"Okay, we can see if she has a chip, and if it's in the system we'll alert the owners. Otherwise, I'd say the old-fashioned way is putting up fliers. Is one of you okay to keep her until she's got a permanent home?" Hattie asks.

"Yes," Jax and I say in unison, then glare at each other. Does she seriously think she's going to keep the cat I found?

TWELVE

Jax

E l looks at me like I've lost my mind, and we both go silent as we glare at each other. She wants to take the cat back home with her to a tiny-ass New York City apartment? That seems crazy. I know cats aren't like dogs, but they should at least have some room to roam around. We agree to discuss it on the way home, and Hattie seems satisfied with the answer to release the cat to us.

"We just need a name for her, for chart purposes," Hattie explains.

"Mistletoe," El says, and when I give her a weird look, she goes on, "Because she had mistletoe in her foot, and I don't know, I did find her in the snow."

"Cute." I actually like the name—I'm just surprised someone who seems to hate the holidays and anything nice thought of it.

El says goodbye to her friends as I follow Hattie to her office to get Mistletoe and a cat carrier. We ditch the box, and she even gives us a few free samples of cat food and treats she keeps on hand. It is enough for the next few days, but we'll have to get some more. Hattie checks, and since Mistletoe isn't chipped, we'll have to put up signs or post in the town's Facebook group to make sure she isn't a missing cat. But with how small Evergreen is, I know if she was missing, there would be a notice up within an hour.

"You really think you're taking her home?" El says when we get in the car. Her friends wave goodbye to us, but they can't hear us argue.

"Well, I would think so, yeah."

"You can't even take care of your business, but you want to take care of a pet?" El says sassily. I grip the steering wheel tightly as I drive.

"You think the city is a better place? I know it's full of mice and rats for her to play with, but don't you think she should have more than a few inches of space in your apartment to play?" I scoff.

"Is that what you think of the city?" She laughs. "Of course it is—you're such a townie."

"What's that supposed to mean?"

"You've lived in a small town your whole life, right? And you think anywhere with more people is scary and dirty. When in reality, you're the one living in a shoebox of a town," El explains with a mocking tone.

"Just because someone lives in a small town doesn't mean they'll stay there forever," I grumble.

"Oh yeah? And when's the last time you traveled outside of this little day trip? Ever been to another country? Ever been on a plane? Have you even been to New York City outside of Times Square and Central Park?" She laughs.

I stay silent. Because no, I haven't done any of those things. But I don't feel like admitting that to her right now.

"See what I mean." She shakes her head at me. "You don't even know how it is in the city because you've never let yourself experience it."

"So show me," I challenge her.

"What?" She's taken aback by my reply.

"Show me. If you really think I'm some 'townie,' then show me how the other side lives. Then we can see who Mistletoe is better suited for." I shrug. She's quiet, so I glance over my shoulder at her—she's deep in thought, the lines on her forehead squishing together.

"How would I even show you? Like, you'd come to the city?" she asks.

"Sure." There's no way she'll actually go through with it, so I don't feel I have anything to lose.

"Fine."

Wait, what? My head snaps around to look at her—she isn't laughing or anything. She's being serious.

"You're going to show me the city?" I ask, making sure I hear her correctly.

"Yes, why not? Come see how I live. My apartment is big enough." She shrugs.

"You want me to stay with you?"

"How else would you see how I live? You'll be surprised, and then you'll be begging me to take Mistletoe off your hands," she says smugly.

I think she's bluffing, but I'm not one hundred percent sure. If I say yes and she folds, then I win, but if she's not and I say yes, then I'm stuck staying at her place. After a day like today, when all I want to do is push her against a wall, tear her clothes off, and eat her out, I don't think that's a good idea. But I'm not about to back down from a challenge either.

"Deal, but only because I'm sure that you'll be the one doing the begging." I smirk. El blushes, and I know I've got her right where I want her.

The following weekend, I take the train down to the city. I want to drive, but after El tells me that I'll either need to pay over $100 for the night or spend forever looking for a parking spot, I decide against it. The rules are simple: I am to spend the night at her apartment, and she'll show me New York City things, proving how there aren't "rats and garbage everywhere," while we both agree not to talk about the eviction notice or the bookstore. Hopefully that will limit our usual arguments.

When I get off the train at Grand Central, I'm immediately overwhelmed. It's loud, there are people everywhere, and I have no idea where I'm going. I stop to glance at the ceiling, and someone pushes me out of the way. I almost go flying into someone else, and when I try to apologize, they scoff and call me a "stupid tourist." So far, I'm not impressed. But El tells me to meet her at the big clock in the middle of Grand Central, and I'm looking around for it. Surprisingly, I spot El first.

She's wearing bright red tights, a black skirt, and a red sweater. She has on her usual black peacoat over her outfit and a pair of black ankle boots. She's standing next to the clock and looking around the room slowly. She hasn't spotted me yet, so it gives me a minute to take all of her in. It becomes more obvious to me that I'm not going to be able to ignore this crush of mine. Maybe if she weren't such a good kisser, or if I could just ignore how badly I want to be crushed by those thighs of hers…

I push away all those thoughts as she looks my way, and I wave at her. She lights up, a smile crossing her face, but just as quickly she controls her face. Is it possible she is fighting feelings like I am?

"Hey," I say as I cross what feels like an ocean of people to get to her.

"Hi. Train okay?" she asks.

"Yup. I did get yelled at and called a tourist once I got here, though."

"Well, were you looking at the ceiling and walking slowly?" she looks at me knowingly.

I open my mouth to argue but then nod with a sigh.

"If you don't want to be called a tourist, don't act like one." She laughs. "Come on, the subway is this way."

"The subway?"

"Yeah, how else would we get to my apartment?" she says.

"Uber? Isn't that how all New Yorkers move around?" I say sheepishly.

"Maybe the rich ones, but real New Yorkers who aren't willing to spend an arm and a leg during rush hour take the subway." El leads us down the side of Grand Central, we go down a flight of stairs, and we walk a few minutes until we get to the subway turnstile.

"Do you have Apple Pay set up?" she asks.

"Uh, yeah?" I take out my phone but grip it tightly.

She laughs. "No one is going to rob your phone. Tap to pay for the subway," she explains.

"Oh." She does it first, and I copy her and walk through the turnstile, following her to our train.

It's hot in the subway; I fan my face, but it doesn't seem to help. She's walking faster than I anticipate, which isn't helping with the heat. Why is it seven million degrees down here when it's freezing out? I tug off my scarf and shove it in my bag. We get on the four-train uptown, and it's insanely crowded. El's body is pressed against mine; I'm holding my bag with one hand and my other is on one of the silver poles. I can feel El's breath and smell her lavender perfume—among a million other scents. I glance up, and she's staring at me; she licks her lips slowly, and I swallow hard.

The train conductor says something, but it sounds like muffled noise. At the next stop, I look to El for direction, but she doesn't say anything, so I guess it isn't our stop. More people attempt to get on even though the subway car is packed. People are pushing and shoving worse than before, and I get pushed closer to El. She laughs quietly when I look startled by the chaos.

She leans in close, and I gulp. "Do we need to head back to Grand Central already?" she asks smugly.

"No," I say breathlessly. I can handle all the people—what I can't handle is El. I should've used my vibrator before I came on this adventure. Then maybe I wouldn't be as horny as I am right now.

Three stops later, we attempt to get off the train. I say "excuse me," but no one hears me, so El takes my hand and pulls me through the chaos. People give her a pissed-off look, but if she cares, she doesn't show it. She doesn't let go of my hand until we're on the street, and I feel a cool breeze from the winter air.

"God, I thought I was going to melt in there," I admit.

"They always put the heat on in the winter even though it really doesn't need it," El explains. "Come on, my apartment is this way."

I look around at all the tall buildings. The city is intimidating. I remember taking a school field trip to the Museum of Natural History when I was a kid, and it feels the same. Somehow, I was just as small compared to the buildings as I am now. El waves me on, and I catch up with her. Her building looks newer than I anticipated, and it actually has an elevator. I always thought that every New Yorker had an apartment on the fiftieth floor with no elevator.

El unlocks the door to her apartment, 14A, and it's beautiful. She takes off her shoes and places them on a shoe rack by the door, so I do the same. Dropping my bag next to them, I follow her as she shows me around. The first space is the living room and kitchen together—one side for each—with huge, floor-to-ceiling windows on the kitchen side. The view is breathtaking, not that I'll admit that. How the hell is this a real place? Clearly she is using her family's money to pay for this place.

"You like the view, don't you?" El stands behind me.

"It's okay." I shrug like it's no big deal, even though inside I'm impressed. I can see the Empire State Building and some of Central Park.

"It has two bedrooms and a full bath, and you'll be happy to know I've never even seen a roach." She smirks.

"Yet there are no Christmas decorations?" I ask, looking at

the surprisingly bare apartment. There are less than two weeks until Christmas. Why doesn't she have anything up yet?

"Oh, well, I work a lot." She shrugs.

"So do I, but I still have a tree and decorations everywhere."

"I live by myself, so it doesn't seem necessary this year." She frowns, looking around.

"That's sad."

"Don't tell me you live alone and still decorate everything?"

"I don't live alone, but even if I didn't live with my grandma, I'd still decorate. It looks like someone forgot to bring your holiday cheer." I sigh.

"You live with your grandma?" she asks.

"Yeah, she's raised me since my parents died," I admit.

"Oh, I didn't know."

"It's okay. My grandma and I are close, she—" I stop myself, realizing I'm going to talk about the bookstore.

"Anyway, since you aren't impressed yet by my very clean apartment and beautiful view, I guess we'll have to have some New York food." She smiles.

"Like what?" I raise an eyebrow.

"Literally anything. I have a taco place, a diner, pizza, Thai, Chinese, and sushi all within walking distance of my apartment. Or we can DoorDash if you don't want to go outside again." She laughs.

"What would a New Yorker do? I feel like all New York City shows have people eating bagels."

"Bagels are for breakfast. Everyone knows the good bagel shops are already closed for the day by now. You want them fresh, first thing in the morning," she explains.

"Okay, fine, then I guess pizza sounds good," I say.

"Get your coat on—the best place is just down the block."

El slides back into her boots and gears up for the weather. She slips a wallet and her phone into her jacket pocket and waits for me to do the same. She locks the door behind us, and we venture outside. I have my eyes peeled for rats and robbers. Both of which are high on my list to avoid.

"Would you relax? You look like you're tweaking." She shakes her head. "You're going to be fine."

"Okay." I don't know why, but when she says it, I start to feel it.

El starts talking about how good the pizza is—how she tried it when she first moved here with her friend Bells. They stumbled upon it drunk one night, and when they came back sober, they were happy it was just as delicious. She's going on and on about her friend and this pizza, but I'm only watching her lips and the way they curve as she speaks. They are painted a dark red today, her white teeth shining brightly behind them. Her light brown hair flows behind her down her back, a few loose strands threatening to get stuck in her lipstick but somehow never do.

I'm mesmerized by her—so much so that I don't even realize we're at the place. El orders for me and turns me down when I offer her cash, insisting I find us a table and some napkins instead. The pizza grease drips down my chin, and I wipe it up as El laughs. But she's right—this is the best pizza. It's cheesy, the sauce is sweet, and the crust is the perfect combination of chewy and crunchy.

THIRTEEN

El

____

I can't believe it was my idea to go ice skating, but when Bells reminded me, how could I say no? We went all the time during winter breaks from college. It's something I'm surprisingly good at because of my balance. Bells, on the other hand, is a disaster who is always falling on her ass. But we both have such a good time that we never care who is better. We get looks from the front gate every time we enter because of our size. How could two overweight women go ice skating? But then I enjoy the looks on everyone's faces when they realize I'm actually really good. I know what I'm doing, and my balance from years of yoga helps. It has been a bit since I have time to go to a yoga class, so I'm not sure how good I'll be. But it is definitely a New York bucket-list item to go ice skating at Rockefeller Center.

"You know I can go ice skating in Evergreen, right?" Jax says when I tell her what we're doing today.

"Yes, but not surrounded by hundreds of people, nor can you in the middle of the city. It's beautiful, and they play music, and people gather around up top to watch. It's a lot of fun." I smile.

"Something you actually enjoy? I didn't think that was something you had in you, Gomez." Jax winks.

"Hey! Stop calling me that," I grumble.

"Holy shit, did you actually read the book? Or did you just Google it?" Jax looks at me quizzically.

"Well, now I wish I did that." I laugh. "I've read about half so far, and I can assure you I'm not Gomez."

I picked up the book after finding it in my suitcase. I didn't intend to read it, but I also don't want to keep being called a character I know nothing about. So I started reading, and it's surprisingly good. Gomez, although a male name, is actually a female character's last name. She is the antagonist who hates Christmas, loves money, and only wants to ruin the town. It isn't a fun thing to find out that that's how Jax sees me.

"Wow, I'm impressed. I figure you threw the book away."

"I thought about it, but curiosity got the better of me." I shrug.

"It is kind of hard to convince me you're not Gomez when you don't even decorate for Christmas." Jax shrugs as she puts on her coat.

I frown. It isn't like I haven't thought about it, but with me working so much and spending time in Evergreen, it doesn't seem necessary. I don't care if there are decorations or not, and it isn't like anyone else is here. Tara has moved most of her stuff out, just a few things hanging behind in the closets. It seems like a more permanent break this time, and I'm not necessarily upset about that. I feel a tiny bit of relief knowing there is a chance this is done for good. We haven't spoken since we decide to take the break, so I have no idea what she is thinking or doing.

Last night Jax spent the night in the guest room. We stay up late watching a classic New York movie, *When Harry Met Sally*. It isn't my favorite, but it's iconic, and we agree on that. Jax and I spend a lot of the movie talking anyway. Getting to know each other's favorite things, talking about our dreams and plans for the future. It is unexpected, but I actually am having a nice time with her. As long as I ignore the burning tension I feel between us.

We take the six-train to Rockefeller Center, grab ice skates, and head for the ice. I'm all bundled up with winter gear, and Jax looks terrified. She's wearing the skates, but she's afraid to stand up. Laughing, I take her hand and pull her toward the ice. It won't be so bad once we get out there. I let go once I give her a hand to the railing, and I skate away, my feet gliding on the ice under me. I go with the crowd, making sure not to go in the wrong direction. They are sticklers about that.

"Wait for me!" Jax calls, and all of a sudden, she's catching up to me. I'm surprised—she's actually pretty good despite her hesitation.

We spend hours gliding along the ice. Watching families guide little ones and couples holding hands. There's Christmas music playing from the speakers above and tourists peeking down at us from above. We can see the huge Christmas tree, and I tell Jax it's probably from somewhere near Evergreen Valley. They usually get it from a northeastern state and drive it down in early December. I don't make a habit of going to the tree lighting—way too many people—but I do see it sometimes on my way home from work.

By the time we're done skating, we're both exhausted. We grab sushi from a nearby place and carry it back to my apartment. The subway is crowded since it's a Saturday, but at least it's not as hot today. Jax looks happier than I've ever seen her, and I wonder if it's me or the city that's growing on her. I'm too afraid of the answer to ask. She helps carry the food in as I open my apartment's door.

"Why don't you open everything? I'm gonna take a quick shower," I tell her.

"You don't want me to wait?"

"Nah, I have to wash my hair, so you might as well dig in," I assure her.

Heading to the bathroom, I grab everything I need for my shower. I even shave my legs, not that I think anything is happening tonight, but I hate the way leg hair feels when it grows out. Sometimes it tickles my legs, and that is a sensory nightmare. After my shower I wrap my extra-long towel around my body and realize I forgot clothes. Holding the towel tightly, I sneak across the hall to my bedroom. Looking down the hall to make sure Jax isn't coming out of the kitchen, I pause, then turn and—

"Oof!" I'm slammed into a hard body, and we both go crashing to the floor.

"What are you doing here?!" I yell, scrambling to get up, but my hands are too wet to get a good grip.

"You invited me!" Jax yells back.

"I mean in the hall! I thought you were in the kitchen!" I exclaim, holding my towel and standing up.

"I needed my phone charger," Jax says, holding up the white cord in her hand.

"Oh." I glare at her even though it's just as much my fault as hers.

She looks at me, then her eyes drop, pop open, and her cheeks redden.

"What?" I say angrily when I glance down and realize my entire left tit has popped out of my towel. I've been standing here yelling at her with it out. "Oh my God!" I scramble to cover myself up, and Jax gulps.

We both head in opposite directions. I get dressed and have to force myself to leave my bedroom. It is no big deal—she has tits, she's seen tits, it's fine. Although I don't believe it myself, I force myself out of the bedroom. She's quietly eating sushi at the kitchen table, and I wonder if I should say something. What would I even say? Sorry you saw my boob? I know it's an accident, but it isn't a hardship to have seen them. They're both nice, really nice. If anything, she should be thanking me.

My phone buzzes, taking my attention away from everything. Paige sent a photo of her and Mistletoe, with the caption "aunt duties going great." Paige is holding Mistletoe, who is wearing a Santa hat. Mistletoe doesn't look thrilled, but she's wearing it, so I guess she doesn't hate it. I bring my phone over to Jax to show her.

"That's so cute," Jax says, just as another text pops up on the top of the screen. I almost die of mortification as I read it.

BELLS: how's it going with your Christmas hottie? Y'all bang yet?

What makes it worse is the series of emojis after it.

BELLS:

I'm going to kill Bells.

"Looks like you should text her back. Don't want to keep her waiting," Jax says, cracking up.

"I don't know why she said any of that, I swear," I say, my cheeks as red as Santa's hat.

"Sure," Jax says sarcastically, "like you haven't been talking about me to your bestie."

"I might've been talking about you, but I definitely wasn't using those emojis." I scoff.

"Right, I'm sure you didn't tell her about our makeout session in the closet." Jax smirks.

"What are you, fifteen? I don't text my best friend every time I make out with someone," I lie. Of course I text her. As soon as I get home that night, Bells has all the details.

Jax stands up and leans in close to my ear. I can feel her breath on it. "You should never play poker; you're a terrible liar."

I suck in a breath. Why the hell is she so close to me? And how does she always seem to smell like Christmas?

"I guess it's okay; I don't kiss and tell anyone either." She winks.

"Maybe we can keep this between us too, then." And before she can ask, I'm pulling her in by the waist and kissing her.

For a second she's startled, but then she's wrapping her arms around my neck and kissing me back. There are quick pecks against her lips that turn into more. Her bottom lip juts out, and I nibble on it, pulling it toward me and watching her groan. I pick her up, and she gasps as I place her on the kitchen table and stand between her thighs. She weighs almost nothing, and all I want to do is lay her down. She hooks her legs around my waist as we kiss, and her hands travel to my chest. I'm not wearing a bra, just an old hoodie and a pair of sweatpants. I haven't even bothered to put on a cute pair of panties. This is the last thing on my mind when I got dressed.

"Fuck," she mutters against my lips when she realizes there's only one layer between her and my breasts. "Tell me I can take this off."

"Yes, please." I moan.

She puts my arms up and slowly pulls the sweatshirt over my head. Halfway, she stops to admire my breasts before taking it off completely and tossing it aside. Her head dips, and she takes one of my nipples in her mouth. Tugging on it with her teeth, she squeezes and plays with the other one. I watch as she looks up at me with dark eyes, smirking as she pulls the other one between her fingers.

"Yesss." I whimper. It has been too long since I've been touched like this. Every nerve ending in my body is on fire right now.

"God, I fucking love your body," she whispers in my ear before biting my neck. She sucks on it gently, careful not to leave a mark, and I moan.

Jax's movements are careful and delicate. She touches my stomach with desire and care. She isn't brushing over it the way some do, or ignoring it completely the way others might. She takes the time to study my body and all of its assets. Only making me want her even more. God, it's going to be embarrassing when she takes my pants off.

She leans back on the table, and because of my height, my pussy is at the same height as her knee. Noticing this, she moves me so my pussy is directly aligned with her knee. She moves it ever so slightly, causing me to gasp.

"God, you must be so fucking wet for me. Aren't you?" she

whispers in my ear. It sounds more like a threat, but what does it say about me that that only turns me on more?

"Maybe," I lie.

"Seriously, sweetheart, you should never play poker." She chuckles to herself. "Now ride my fucking knee."

"Yes, ma'am." I nod.

Grinding my pussy against her feels like torture. It is a small fraction of what I want right now. But I'm not about to argue with her. If she wants to take control, then I'm going to let her. She has both her hands on my breasts, and I'm moaning as my clit connects with her knee. Her lips are on my neck, and I whimper as I slide my hips back and forth on her. Why the hell is this so hot? We are basically dry humping, yet I'm embarrassingly close to finishing on her lap.

I reach for her chest, pulling her sweater over her head. Tossing it aside, I take off her bra too and tug hard on her nipples, pulling both of them at once, causing her to moan loudly for me.

"Oh, fuck!" she cries, head falling back in pleasure.

I slide my hand down her chest, her tight stomach, and place my palm on her pussy. Jax's head snaps back, looking directly at me as I leave my hand there. When I place just a small amount of pressure, she groans. I swivel my hips, grinding harder than before, causing a moan of my own.

"Oh, fuck, you're going to come, aren't you?" she realizes, locking in on my moans.

"Mmm," I whimper. Grinding my clit directly against the top of her knee has me hanging on the edge.

"Come for me, beautiful, and I might just fuck that pussy myself," Jax whispers in my ear. Pulling my hair back, gripping tightly, I grind one last time and let myself go completely.

"Oh! Yes! Yes! Yes!"

But instead of the orgasm I'm chasing, I feel a different sensation. It's almost like I'm going to pee, and suddenly I'm gushing all over her lap as I moan out her name. "Jax! Yes! Oh, Jax!"

"Holy hell," Jax praises, and I jump up, realizing the mess I've made.

"I'm so freaking sorry." I've squirted before, but never like this; it's like it completely took over me. Standing up makes me feel a little dizzy until Jax grabs my hand.

She uses her other hand to pull my face toward hers. "Never apologize for making a mess; I'm more than happy to clean up. Besides, it gives me a good reason to take my pants off."

FOURTEEN

Jax

I stand up, tossing my pants aside and watching as El realizes her pants are just as much of a mess as mine. She tugs them off, grabs mine, and disappears. For a few moments, I wonder if she's hiding out because she's embarrassed or something. But then she comes out just as naked as before and smiles.

"Sorry about that; I put them in the washer, so they should be done later," she explains.

She has a washing machine in her apartment too? That shit is unheard of. I have to hide how impressed I am.

"No worries. Do you want to continue? Maybe in the bedroom?" I suggest.

"I'd like that." She nods. Her smile is soft, the sides of her mouth curved slightly, as she leads me to her room.

It's the first time I'm seeing it, so I want to take it all in. It has lavender walls with huge windows and all-black furniture. The bed is at least a queen, with nightstands on each side. There are clothes on the floor next to the bed and a lamp in the corner of the room. I turn, and El is waiting for me on the bed—her body posed like that famous "paint me like one of your French girls" meme. All of her curves are currently making her look like a

Greek goddess. Her thighs are begging to have my face in between them. I climb into the bed next to her, only in my boy shorts, my hard nipples making it impossible to hide how turned on I am. I mean, having a sexy woman finish on my lap is one way to do it.

"Is there anything you don't want to do?" I ask. We sort of jumped into whatever this is headfirst, and I don't want to overstep a boundary I don't know about.

"I'm not into getting my ass eaten, or ass stuff in general, but otherwise everything goes. What about you?" El says.

"The same—and, uh, no feet. It's cool if that's your thing, but I don't wanna suck on your toes or have you suck on mine."

"Not my thing, but also not kink-shaming," El says with a laugh.

With that out of the way, I lean in to kiss her. Our lips collide, and her tongue swirls around my mouth, jolting something inside me. Watching her literally squirt all over my lap isn't something I knew I wanted, but now that I've had it, I never want anything else. El pulls me closer to her, nudging my thighs apart with her knee. She moves her knee between my legs and pushes it against my pussy. I'm still wearing boy shorts, but I know she can feel how wet I currently am. I mean, who wouldn't be? El is naked, her body dripping in curves, intoxicating as she twists it around me.

El kisses my neck, dragging her tongue along the slope of it. Holy fuck, her tongue is warm against my cool skin, and I groan. She switches between licking and nibbling at my neck. Her hands reach for my bare chest, and I moan as she grabs my breasts in her hands. They are on the smaller side and fit almost perfectly. I've always loved being on the smaller side. I can fit into most shirts, and I never have to worry about a bra unless I want one.

She knocks her knee against my center, and I gasp. I run my hands down her waist and pull her closer. She drops her head between my breasts and places wet kisses down my chest and stomach, all the way to the top of my underwear. Her breath hitches as she smells my arousal. My underwear is sticking to me, my wetness making it impossible to hide how much I want her. El kisses the top of my underwear and dips her hand inside.

"Mmm," I hum as she bumps her hand into my clit.

"I'm going to fuck you with my fingers until you come, screaming my name," El whispers in my ear.

I don't have a chance to reply, because her hand is curving and a finger slips inside me. Gasping, I wrap my legs around hers. She giggles, kissing my skin as she moves her finger in and out of me torturously slow. Is it going to be like this? I move my hips against her hand, dying for a little more friction, and she giggles again.

"Do you want more?" she bats her eyelashes at me, and I nod quickly.

She moves her hand out and then slips another finger inside me. With her free hand, she works on tugging my underwear off and tossing them aside. I can feel her breath on my pussy, my ass on her silk sheets, and her fingers curling inside me. I reach for my clit, and, after wetting my fingers, I draw slow circles around it. I know what I like and what I desperately need. El watches as her fingersw slip inside me and I play with myself. She looks mesmerized as my pussy takes her fingers in and out, her hand dripping with my desires. I want to tell her not to stop, to keep going, but it's impossible for me to speak. I'm looking at this gorgeous woman, and I'm actually tongue-tied.

Her hair falls all around her, thick strands of auburn contrasting with her light skin. Her eyes bore into mine, and I moan. I didn't think this would be happening—I mean, sure, I sort of hoped—but I didn't plan it. I have packed something just in case, but I didn't want to be the one to initiate anything. I figured if it was meant to be, it would happen whenever it happened. Thinking about what I brought and using it with her only pushes me closer to the edge.

"Fuck! Right there!" I cry out, and my orgasm rushes over me.

El doesn't stop until I'm pushing her fingers away and I'm collapsing into the bed. She places soft kisses down my neck and lies next to me. I can feel her fingers lazily drawing circles on my stomach as I catch my breath. My whole body is buzzing; I feel like I could equally run a marathon and sleep for three days.

"I want to get something, but I don't want you to read too much into it," I say, turning to El, and she raises an eyebrow at me.

"Okay…" she says, and I run to the guest room. Grabbing it from my suitcase in the secret pocket, I return, and El gasps as I take it out from behind my back.

"So you just happen to bring that with you?" she smirks.

"Would you believe me if I said I normally keep it in my suitcase?" I lie.

"Nope." She giggles. "But I'm sort of glad you brought it."

"Oh yeah?" I toss the strap onto the bed, and El grabs it. She picks it up, examining it and holding it in her hands. I know I don't have a dick, but if I did, with the way she is holding it, I definitely would be hard.

"Can you use it on me?" she asks, blushing. Her cheeks are a light pink as she chews on her bottom lip.

"I'd fucking love to use it on you." I nod. When I pick it up, El keeps her eyes on me as I slide the strap into place. It's at least ten inches and thick all around, but it's bright red. Something hard to hide, and it's my biggest fear my grandma might one day find it.

"Well, what are you waiting for?" El smirks, and I climb back onto the bed.

I kiss her lips briefly before going down on her. El gasps as I lay my tongue against her clit. It's throbbing, her pussy still dripping and ready for me. I swirl my tongue around her clit and hold on tightly to her thighs as I do. She pushes my head down, twisting her fingertips in my curls. A beautiful woman pulling my hair will always get me hotter.

I feel El's breathing start to change, and instead of letting her come on my face, I pull back. I spread her delicious thighs apart and line up the strap at her center. "You're in control; just let me know what you need," I tell her.

"Okay," she whispers. Her eyes are on me as I slide the tip of it inside her. Pushing in slowly, giving her a second to adjust, she moans out in pleasure. "Oh, yes!"

"More, baby?" I ask.

"Oh, yes, please!"

I push my hips forward, the strap going in farther, and watch as El's face twists in pleasure. I tilt my body toward hers and listen to the sounds of her pussy crying for me. She's so wet that I'm in danger of falling out of her. Pushing into her and pulling out in a rhythm, I listen to her whimpers to figure out what she likes. Her eyes are closed; she tries to keep them open as long as she can. Her body moves, twisting as she bucks her hips toward mine to get more friction. I rake my thumb over her clit, teasing it gently.

"Fuck! I'm so sensitive!" El cries as I pound into her and keep my thumb on her clit.

"Good, I wanna see you come for me again." I smirk.

There is nothing like fucking a woman. I don't know how there are men out there who don't enjoy pleasuring their women. I would do this all damn day if I could. El pulls me in for a kiss, causing me to collapse on top of her. Her puckered nipples brush against my stomach, and I groan. Her lips devour mine as I pound my hips into her. She stops kissing me and wraps her arms around me, holding my body tightly against hers as she starts to come. El is gasping as her thighs start to shake, and she's moaning my name in my ear.

"That's it, baby; I want you to come. Be so good and finish for me," I whisper in her ear.

"Oh, yes! Jax! Fuck! Fuck! Yes!"

Her body relaxes; her arms unwrap from my body, and I carefully pull out of her. The strap is dripping with her juices, so I climb closer to her head and tell her, "Suck me clean."

El's dark eyes shoot open, and she gasps before taking the strap in her mouth. I watch as she sucks and licks it clean. Her tongue swirls down the length and then around the base. She takes a good portion of it down her throat and cleans the rest with her tongue. Once it's clean, she stops, and I lie on the bed next to her. I lean in and kiss her lips softly.

"Wow." Her breathing is still uneven.

"Wow indeed." I smile. I love knowing what kind of reaction I can coax out of her.

"I need a moment to catch my breath, and then it's your turn," she tells me.

"Oh yeah?"

"If you want, yes," she quickly says.

"I'd be honored to have your tongue wherever you'd like to put it." I wink.

El sits up, has a sip of water, and offers me some. I shake my head, and then she looks at me expectantly. "I want you to sit on my face."

"The queen's throne? My pleasure." I nod.

"Mmm, whenever you're ready." El positions herself a little lower on the pillows so I have room to sit.

El doesn't have a headboard, so there's nothing to grip as I slide my legs apart and lean over her face. Looking down at her bright red lips and dark eyes smiling at me, I relax as I lower my pussy over her. She hums against me, and I groan, my hands palms out on the wall. She wraps her arms around my thighs and holds me steady as she begins to eat me out. Her tongue consumes me, slipping up and down my folds as she lavishes me. I can feel the vibrations of her moans as she tastes me. There is nothing hotter than someone who enjoys the way you taste. It completely ruins the vibe when someone goes down on you because they feel they have to. Someone going down on you because they want to? Absolutely nothing better.

I rock my hips back and forth over El's lips and tongue. I'm still sensitive from earlier, and I know it won't take me long. I try to hold myself up as best as I can, but as soon as my orgasm hits, I'm toppling over her. My legs shake, going limp, and I can barely hold myself up as I moan for her.

"Yes! Oh God, El! Please!" I cry out with little pants. She smiles under me until I slide off her completely.

El and I take a moment, lying next to each other to catch our breaths. I try to hold back my yawn, but I am suddenly exhausted. The combination of multiple orgasms and ice skating is taking a toll on me.

"Why don't we get some sleep?" El suggests.

"Okay, I'm going to use the bathroom." I kiss her cheek and head across the hall.

After peeing, I sneak into the guest bedroom, having a feeling I'm not sleeping in there tonight. I reach for my bag of bathroom essentials and take out the toothpaste and my toothbrush. After I brush thoroughly, I place the toothbrush in the cup on the side of the sink. But that's when I notice it: the second toothbrush. I thought she said she lives by herself, but then why are there two toothbrushes in the cup? Maybe one is a new one? It seems like an odd place to put a new toothbrush, but I am clinging to hope. Upon a closer look, they're both clearly used, with old toothpaste under the bristles. I don't know if this is something I should bring up, but I also don't want to be somewhat of another woman. It is clear the other woman doesn't live here; I've been over for almost forty-eight hours, and there's no other indication of her. Maybe it's better if I don't bring it up.

FIFTEEN

El

Jax is a little tense after we have sex, but I'm not sure what changed. One minute she's riding my face, and the next she isn't smiling and her body is tense. I'm afraid to ask her what's wrong, but after I rack my brain, I can't think of anything I've done. It isn't like we didn't have a good time; maybe this is just how she is after sex. Or maybe she regrets it. It hurts to think that way, but we do have a feud going on, so I wouldn't blame her.

"Is everything okay?" I ask, swallowing my anxiety.

"I'm just confused about something." Her mouth forms a line as she looks at me.

"Okay? About what?"

"I saw two toothbrushes in the bathroom. Does someone else live here? Or is someone else staying here?" she asks hesitantly. "It's probably not my business, but I'm not interested in being the other woman."

I sigh; I haven't even noticed that. "You're definitely not the other woman. But there was someone living here not too long ago. My ex, Tara," I explain.

"Oh." She looks like she wants to say more, so I decide to fill in the blanks.

"We took a break a few weeks ago, and then she moved out shortly after. We haven't spoken, and I don't think we will be again. She and I were together for a while, but for the last few years it was pretty complacent, and there was no spark or anything. We fight a lot, and neither of us are happy. I think neither of us want to admit it is over. But it is, and I genuinely didn't notice the toothbrush—I'm not trying to hide anything here," I explain.

"I see." Jax seems to be taking it all in. "I'm not, like, asking because this has to be something, but I don't want to be complicit in helping someone cheat."

"I understand, and you're not. I wouldn't do that, but I also understand why it might look like that. I didn't really anticipate this happening," I admit.

"Neither did I." Jax rubs the back of her neck and chuckles.

"You can ask me anything. I don't want you worried about my ex."

"Nah, it's fine. I just want to make sure, but we're good." Jax nods.

"So, are you coming to bed?" I ask, patting the bed next to me.

"You want me to sleep in here?" She looks surprised.

"I mean, you don't have to. But if you want to…"

"Yeah, let me grab some underwear. I cannot sleep without some." Jax laughs.

"We couldn't be more opposite." I laugh as she heads to the guest room.

I put my phone on the charger, ignoring the messages from Bells. Even though she is sort of the reason behind this hookup. I will give her an update when I know Jax won't see our texts. I don't know exactly what this is between us yet, and I don't want to tell Bells it is something before I'm sure. She will understand, and I have a feeling she knows my lack of reply is just confirmation we are hooking up.

Jax comes back wearing just a pair of black boy shorts, and I internally groan. She looks like a goddamn Calvin Klein model. Why the hell does she have to be so fucking hot? She slides into bed next to me, going under the covers. It isn't freezing in the apartment, but it is a little chilly. I have the comforter and the thick throw blanket over us. She turns to face me, and I tense a little.

Are we going to cuddle? Is that too intimate? Does she even like cuddling? I can't remember the last time I laid next to someone. Tara and I had been sleeping in different beds for months now, and who knows what Jax prefers. Is this just going to be a one-time thing? Or is this actually something? I try to ignore the feeling of knots in my stomach. I know exactly how my family will react if they find out about us. And it will not be a pleasant reaction.

"Are you cool if I put my arm around you? I've been told I'm a sleep cuddler." Jax chuckles.

"Yeah, of course." I smile.

I turn so my back is to Jax, and she wraps her arm across my waist. She pulls me closer into her body, and I relax.

"So maybe the city isn't so bad," Jax whispers as we fall asleep. I don't respond, afraid of what my voice might say.

In the morning, I get out of bed before Jax and jump in the shower. I'm going back to Evergreen with her today. We haven't discussed who will be getting Mistletoe yet, but either way, we need to get her back from my sister. I grab our clothes from the dryer and pick a new outfit from the closet for myself. I wrap myself in a silk robe until I'm ready to get dressed. I'm putting on my makeup and sipping a hot mug of coffee at my vanity when Jax finally wakes up. She sits up, her tits on full display and her nipples hard. I clench my thighs together as she fixes her bed head and smiles at me. Her short curls are in disarray, and she looks beautiful. Do we have time for a quickie before we get the train? I'm afraid of what might happen when we head back to Evergreen Valley.

"Good morning." She smiles and stretches her arms above her head.

"Good morning. Do you want some coffee? Or some break-fast?" I ask.

"I think I was promised a good New York bagel." She smirks.

"We can get that on the way to the train, then?"

"Sounds good." She gets out of bed and heads to the bath-room. I watch her through the vanity mirror, her back muscles on full display. What does she do to get muscles like that?

Jax returns and surprises me by spinning around my vanity chair and pulling me in for a kiss. Her hands don't leave my face as she holds me close. My mind races as she kisses me with fervor. She's still naked, her hardened nipples against my chest. Am I supposed to resist this?

"Let me taste you one last time." She whispers in my ear. One last time? Well, that makes it clear—this must be a one-time thing for her.

"Okay." I nod, wanting to extend this for as long as I can.

Jax drops to her knees and—fuck, what a sight. A woman on her knees, needy and ready for you, should be illegal. She spreads apart my thighs and tugs on the robe's string, letting it fall to the side. I slide my arms out, and it falls to the ground.

"Fuck, you are so fucking sexy." She pushes my stomach back so I can lean on the vanity and she can have a better view of my pussy.

Her tongue connects with my core, and I whimper her name. I can't hide how much I want this. I am going to commit every second to memory. After all, this is the last time. I reach for her nipples, but they're too far, so I settle for her hair, tugging on her curls as she swirls her tongue around my clit.

"Mmm," I hum as she sucks on it gently. She knows exactly what she's doing down there and how to get me going.

Jax slides her hands up the insides of my thighs and grips them tightly. I feel her tongue teasing my clit, sucking on it, then letting it go. Every time I get close, she stops and teases me again. It is getting to be torturous, so I squeeze my thighs together, squishing her head in one place, and tug on her hair.

"Fuck me now." I command, and she sucks hard on my clit, causing me to yelp, "Oh! Yes!"

Jax nibbles, and I'm a waterfall for her. My thighs release as I fall back, my pussy exploding, and I squirt all over Jax's face. I'm too afraid to look, so I keep my eyes clamped shut until I feel her pull back. She's wiping her face clean with the side of my robe, and I'm mortified.

"I'm so sorry—" I start to say, but Jax cuts me off with a kiss.

"Didn't I tell you not to apologize for making a mess?" Jax looks at me sternly.

"Yes." I tilt my head down in embarrassment.

Jax tips my chin and makes me look at her, standing above me. Her arms are on either side of mine, leaning on the vanity behind me. "I'm going to shower. Don't even think about apologizing for finishing on me."

I just nod, using the time she's in the shower to fix my makeup and actually get dressed. My coffee is cold, so I dump it down the sink and gather my things together. I don't need too much for the ride, but I like to be prepared. I'm grabbing stuff for my purse when I head back to my room to get my phone. I walk in and see Jax holding up the book she gave me with a smirk.

"So you do read some." She looks impressed.

"I told you I do," I say, rolling my eyes and grabbing the book from her.

"Yeah, but I don't know if I believed you then," Jax admits.

"And now?"

"Well, you even have a bookmark in there. Which is good, because I don't think I could fuck a heathen who bends the corners of the pages to keep her place." Jax laughs.

"Oh, whatever—let's get going."

I put the book on my dresser and grab my phone like I originally intended. We stop for bagels on the way—poppy with cream cheese for both of us. We take the six-train downtown into Grand Central. It's Sunday midday, so it's crowded, but not as bad as it was Friday night. Jax and I grab our tickets, then wait for the board to tell us which gate to go to. Our train ride back is quiet, both of us probably unsure of what to say. Will things go back to the way they are before? Does this weekend change anything? We never even discussed who will be getting Mistletoe. All we did was have sex and get to know each other.

My phone starts buzzing like crazy when Jax is napping. Pulling it out of my purse, I see it's all texts from Tara, which is extra weird since I haven't heard from her in a few weeks.

TARA: How could you?!

TARA: You couldn't even wait a month?!

TARA: Bringing someone back to the place WE lived?

TARA: how fucking dare you

TARA: Attachment 1 video

TARA: I still have access to the Ring camera

TARA: did you think I wouldn't know about this?

Tara is freaking out, and I'm confused until I press play on the video. It's a Ring recording of Jax coming into the apartment Friday night, and then it cuts to today with both of us leaving. I mean, we left for time in between that, but I guess Tara saw both of us leaving with our stuff today. What the hell is she doing stalking the Ring camera? We aren't together. If we are on a break big enough that she moved out, then how can she be shocked I brought someone over? And it isn't even like that with Jax.

ME: I'm not sure why you're stalking the camera when you moved out…

TARA: I'm not stalking it but it said someone was at my front door and I clicked it. I'm not in the wrong here

ME: Neither am I. We broke up. You moved out. You can't be upset about this.

TARA: You're telling me how to feel?

ME: literally no.

TARA: & we're on a break. But I guess this just shows how much you're willing to get back together

TARA: Seriously, you just stop replying?

I stop answering because I'm not sure what she wants me to say. I know this is supposed to be a break, but it is feeling more and more like it should be permanent. And that isn't something I'm going to say over text while I sit next to the woman I hooked up with all weekend. So I put Tara's messages on Do Not Disturb and put my phone back in my purse. I wake Jax up just before our stop so we have time to gather our things.

"Crap, I have to run into town and check something at the store. Do you think we can meet at your sister's house later to talk about Mistletoe?" Jax asks, looking stressed the second we step off the train.

"Of course. I'll text you the address." I smile.

"Cool, I'll see you later." Jax leans in and kisses my cheek. It's a soft, chaste kiss that leaves a lasting impression on me. I don't know what it means, but I'm smiling like an idiot.

I start walking toward the parking lot Paige says to meet her in when I spot my father. He's angrily rushing toward me, and I stop in my tracks. Fuck—did he seen me getting off the train with Jax? Did he see her kiss me? Maybe it isn't a big deal. Maybe I can convince him of that.

"What the hell is that?" he bellows, standing in front of me.

"What is what?" I play dumb.

"You let that woman kiss you. How could you betray the family like that?" he demands.

"I'm not betraying my family," I say quietly. I hate my father has the ability to make me feel two inches tall.

"If you're with an Evans, then you're betraying the family," he scoffs. The only thing I know is that this has nothing to do with me being with a woman—just this particular woman.

"Dad, I understand it's complicated because of the business—"

"It's not just because of the business. Our rivalry goes past that," he says.

"What does that mean?" He's never mentioned this to me before.

He shuffles me to the side, as if five feet away will give us privacy. "Your grandfather asked out Jax's grandmother. She rejected him, very publicly, and then stole the bookstore property out from under him. He told her about it in confidence. So it's not just about property; it's about your grandfather's pride."

"This decade-long rivalry is because Grandpa got his heart broken and can't get over it?" I ask, my voice dripping with sarcasm. Clearly this has to be some kind of a joke.

"It may not seem like a big deal to you, but this is something important to my father. I will not let him see you with her again. Do you understand? I forbid you from ever dating an Evans."

Jax

"Are you out of your mind? Why would you tell her I'm not with you!" I exclaim to Parker.

"You didn't tell me the plan! I thought I was just supposed to cover for you last night. I thought you were already back in town," Parker says nervously.

"What did you say to her exactly?" I ask.

"Your grandma saw me at the bank, asked where you were, and I said I didn't know. I thought you went home last night. Then she said you didn't, and it got awkward. I said maybe you were with Shiloh, and she said she was going to stop by the toy store to see if that was true," Parker explains.

"Fuck. I didn't want her knowing I was even out of town, but now what am I going to say? I have two friends, and if I'm not with them, then where can I be?" I sigh.

I know it isn't the biggest deal; I am a grown woman. I am almost thirty. But I am still a little afraid of my grandma when she thinks I am in one place. Especially when I am lying about being with our family's worst enemy. I suddenly feel more guilt than I anticipate. In a way, I feel like I am betraying my grandma. It isn't like I want to; I just want to kill these feelings I feel for El. But of course, this weekend only made them worse.

"Why don't you just tell her the truth?" Parker says.

"You want me to tell my grandma that I spent the weekend fucking the enemy of her rival? Oh sure, let me just run her over while I'm at it."

"You what?!" Parker's eyes go wide. I'm glad we're in the safety of my office at the bookstore, or this would be the town's next gossip.

"We spent the weekend hooking up," I admit.

"I knew it was just a ruse—you were going to see her apartment for the sake of a cat. Like, come on, that's such a reach, even for you," Parker scoffs.

"That is why I went there," I insist.

"Sure, sure, and how long did it take to hook up with her?" Parker purses her lips.

"Uh, like a day."

"Exactly. Now, don't get me wrong, I ship the hell out of it. It's like this modern-day Romeo and Juliet thing if they were gay and you guys don't kill yourselves," Parker says.

"Oh, thanks." I roll my eyes. "What am I going to do about Grandma? I'm not ready to tell her where I was."

"Why can't you just tell her you were with someone but not say who? Like you're seeing someone, but you don't wanna talk about it until it's serious."

"Wait, that's actually perfect." Is it really that simple?

"I know, I'm a genius," Parker brags.

"Why don't you catch me up to where we're at with other donations? I know you and Shiloh went to local businesses without me."

"Well, yeah. I figured you could use a weekend off, and you'd be stressing about it if we didn't." She shrugs. "We got everyone in town to agree to donate something except the Monroes, who we obviously didn't bother to ask. Everyone else is happy to help and loves the chance to stand up to the Monroes. They all have your back; they just can't risk their own businesses by doing much more."

"I get that; it's only a matter of time before they go after them. Especially if there's a grudge to be had." I sigh.

Parker goes on to show me the spreadsheet she has created to keep track of all the items. It's extremely well organized, and I'm relieved so much has gotten done in my absence.

When I show up to Paige's house, I expect to go inside, but El is waiting outside with Mistletoe, presumably in the cat carrier. I pull up right to them and jump out to open the doors.

"Are you okay? Were you waiting out here long? I'm sorry, I thought I'd be coming in," I scramble to open the door for her.

"It's fine, I wasn't waiting long." She sighs.

"Did something happen with your sister?" I ask.

"I don't really want to talk about it."

"Okay." I nod. "Where did—"

"I know we're supposed to talk about where Mistletoe is supposed to go, but do you think for tonight we could just stay with you? I don't want to take the train home, and I just had a really bad day," she says, her voice shaky.

"Yeah." I hesitate, trying to figure out if I can sneak El into my part of the house without Grandma noticing. I've done it before with one-night stands, saying I have a roommate who goes to sleep early, so it shouldn't be an issue.

We both get into the car, Mistletoe in the back, and I drive to my house. I pull into the driveway and notice all the lights are off, so there's a good chance my grandma's already in bed. It's only seven-thirty, but that's never stopped her before. I sort of think she might be waiting up for me since she knows I'm back in town but hasn't seen me yet. I stayed as long as I could at the store before I picked up El only because I'm avoiding her a little bit. I don't want to lie to her, so I figure avoiding her is the best option for now. Of course, now I'm not sure what I'll do if she catches a Monroe in her house.

"My grandma is probably sleeping, but my side of the house is separate from hers once we get inside," I explain quietly to El. She nods, and I lead her inside.

There's the first floor that has the kitchen, my grandma's room, the living room, the bathroom, and a guest room. The second floor is basically my space—my bedroom, the library, and my office are up here, along with a room I use for a gym and the bathroom. My grandma can, but often doesn't, bother going up the stairs, so it makes sense to transform upstairs into my own space. Once we get upstairs, I let Mistletoe out and set up a makeshift litter box with the cat litter El brought along and an old shoebox.

"So, do you want to talk about it yet?" I ask as El sits on the edge of my bed.

"I had a fight with my dad, about... well, about a lot of things. And I just don't have it in me to fight with anyone else tonight. That's why I was hoping we didn't have to talk about Mistletoe's living arrangements tonight," she explains.

"I understand." I nod. "Do you just want to go to bed—sleep, I mean—or are you up for something?" I realize I'm putting my foot in my mouth here. "By something I literally mean watching a movie."

"Oh, then yes. I could go for a movie." She smiles.

"Why don't I make us some hot cocoa and we can watch a Christmas movie? Do you have a favorite?" I ask.

"I do." She nods. "But I don't want you to judge me for it."

"Why don't I tell you mine and then you can tell me yours?" I suggest.

"Okay." She smiles.

"*It's a Wonderful Life.*"

"That one is so sad!" She gasps.

"I thought we weren't judging! But you'd have great conversations with my grandma; she hates it too." I sigh.

"I like *Christmas with the Kranks*. I know Tim Allen sucks now, but it's a classic. And the whole running-away-from-Christmas vibe is great," El explains.

"That is a good one." I nod. "I have all the streaming things, so help yourself." I hand her the remote to my TV.

"Do you happen to have any pajamas? Or something? I didn't pack any," she frowns.

"Oh." I pause. I don't know if I'll have anything that would fit her. She and I aren't close to the same size in anything.

"I know it's silly—it's not like you're close to my size—but I figured it couldn't hurt to ask." She shrugs.

"I might have something, just hold on." I head to the other room and check the dresser in the closet.

Inside is a bunch of things from my mother, including a pair of Christmas pajamas that look like they might fit El. I pick them up, smelling the old fabric. It doesn't smell like my mother anymore but keeping them here sort of makes it feel like she is here. I know I don't have to give them to El, and she'll even understand if I tell her about them but can't do it. But for some reason, I feel okay with it. So I carefully close the dresser and bring them to El.

"These are so cute—are these your grandma's?" she asks.

"No, they, uh, actually belonged to my mother," I admit.

"Oh, Jax, if you don't want to—"

"No, no, I'm actually okay. They're just clothes, and they happen to be your size; I'm taking it as a sign." I smile.

"Are you sure?" she asks again.

"I'm positive," I assure her. "I'm going to make some hot cocoa, and I'll be back. Marshmallows and whipped cream, okay?"

"Yes, please."

I walk down the stairs, thankful my grandma can't hear very well. She is fine during the day, but she is a dead sleeper, so I don't have to worry about waking her. I find the hot cocoa packets, two mugs, and get to work. Ten minutes later, I'm balancing two piping-hot mugs with candy canes sticking out the sides while I walk up the stairs. When I reach my bedroom, El is lying in my bed, wearing the pajamas, and the movie is cued up on the TV.

"You look beautiful," I say as I place the mug on my nightstand.

"Thanks. They're actually very comfortable."

We start the movie as I climb onto the bed next to her. I leave a little bit of space, unsure of how close I should be sitting next to her. Is there a rule book when you sleep with the person, but she is also your family's rival? This whole thing feels too complicated for my liking, but it isn't like I was going to say no when she asked to come over. She seems to be having a really rough day, and I don't want to add to it by sending her home on the train.

"Thank you," El whispers halfway through the movie.

"For what?" I look at her, confused.

"Hanging out with me. I know this is complicated, but I had a terrible day, and for some reason the only person I want to be with is you," she says softly.

"Really?" My heart quickens as I look at her.

She only nods, like she is afraid of her own voice.

"I'm sorry for whatever happened with your family. I get things can be complicated."

"I just wonder sometimes how much I'm doing things for my family that are hurting what could be good for me." She plays with the edge of the comforter.

"I wonder the same thing," I admit. It is like we are both playing with fire, but neither of us wants to admit it.

"Meow!"

Mistletoe jumps onto the bed, jolting both of us out of our thoughts. It is probably for the best. No matter what happens here, someone is bound to get hurt. Our families have been rivals for such a long time; it's not like they'll magically get over it. I know my grandma will eventually be okay, but I don't want to add to her burden of stress either. At her age, any stress isn't good.

El and I settle back into watching the movie when she scoots a little closer. Her body touches mine, and I can feel the heat of her skin through the thin fabric of her pajamas. I tense. I try not to think about how not even twenty-four hours ago I had her thighs wrapped around my head. I thought that was going to be our last time. I thought it was a one-time thing, and things would go back to the way they were. It's not like El and I have a real future. It is just some built-up tension that we let explode. Except, right now, all I'm thinking about is the way her body reacts to mine and how good she feels when I touch her.

El must feel it too, because when she looks at me, I can feel the passion burning. I want to push her onto the bed, drag off all her clothes, and have her screaming my name. I try to look away, but instead El pulls me in for a kiss. Her tongue drags itself across my closed lips until I open for her. My lips spread like her thighs did earlier. Only after she moans in my mouth do I pull back.

"What are we doing, El?" I ask, her forehead pressed against mine. Both of us are out of breath. Both of us dying to do more than kiss.

"I don't know. What if, for tonight, it doesn't matter?" she whispers.

"Just for the night?" I ask.

"Just for the night," she repeats.

Before I can talk myself out of it, I'm pulling El toward me. Mistletoe meows and jumps off the bed—we're probably moving around too much for her. El climbs onto my lap, and I take her face in my hands. Her hair is everywhere as she rocks her hips against mine. She moans softly into my mouth as I tug on her bottom lip. I can feel her hardened nipples under her braless shirt, the fullness of her breasts drawing me in.

I tug the shirt off over her head and watch as her breasts fall, catching them in my hands. I squeeze and grab at them while her lips are on my neck. I'm holding back moans as I tug on her nipples. El bites down on the side of my neck as I tease her. I slide one hand down the front of her pants, cupping her pussy from the outside and feeling how hot she is. She is like a sauna down there; I can only imagine how wet she is. I slide a hand into her panties, and she lets out a moan.

"You have to be quiet," I say in her ear.

Just because my grandma is a dead sleeper doesn't mean I want her to hear us. God forbid she wake up to pee or something. I would die of mortification if she caught me having sex. All I need is for my grandma to catch me, tongue deep in Eliora Monroe.

SEVENTEEN

El

I'm topless on Jax when she slides a hand in my panties. Then she has the nerve to chastise me for moaning. Like, sorry for being turned on beyond control. Over the weekend we could be as loud as we wanted, and we soaked up every second of that. I'm not used to having to control my moans, so this is definitely an experience for us. I bite down on the side of her neck, presumably leaving a hickey, when she slides her fingers across my clit. How else am I supposed to stay quiet when she does that?

"Such a naughty girl, don't know if you'll make it on the nice list at this rate," Jax mumbles in my ear. I don't know why that's turning me on; it's something I'll have to save for my therapist to figure out. Because Jax is sliding her hand into my panties, and her fingers glide across my wetness like butter on a hot pan.

"God, you're really so wet for me already? What a naughty girl." She can talk, but I can't make a peep; how is this fair?

Jax dips a finger inside me, and my hips buck into her hand. She smirks, liking the way my body reacts to hers. There is no hiding how badly she turns me on. It's primal, the way my body reacts when she is near me. Jax grips my ass with one hand as the fingers of her other curl inside me. I fall against her chest, holding back my moans.

"Mmm, that's a nice girl." She praises my silence.

Jax rewards me by adding a second finger, and I bite my lip again. This time she starts to kiss my neck while she fingers me, and I'm clutching onto her for dear life. I sink into her neck, inhaling her peppermint-and-pine smell. It has to be some kind of body soap she uses that's so fragrant. I kiss the side of her neck to muffle my moans as she fingers me, her palm bumping against my clit each time she pulls back. It is like a bomb getting ready to explode, each accidental touch only bringing the count-down closer.

"Be a nice girl and come on my hand for me," she whispers in my ear.

Keeping her fingeres inside me, she removes her other hand from my ass and uses it to hold my hips. She rocks them against herself, and I'm gasping. My breathing is labored, and all I want to do right now is scream her name. But I'm doing my best to be quiet, so I bite down on the side of her neck again. I don't even know if it's in the same place, and I don't care. If she wants me to be quiet, she'll have to deal with it tomorrow.

My orgasm overpowers me, and I quietly whimper into her neck. Jax keeps her fingers going until I have the strength to push her hand away. Falling into her bed, I collapse breathlessly onto the pillows. Looking up at Jax, I find her smiling, and I have the urge to throw a pillow at her, but I don't have the willpower.

"Why are you smiling?" I grumble.

"Because you're hot when I take your breath away." She smirks.

"If I could throw something at you, I would." I glare at her.

Jax laughs. "I'm sorry, was that not satisfactory? Because I have the bite marks that say otherwise."

"Oh, whatever." I roll my eyes.

"Do you want some water?" Jax asks, and I nod.

She disappears into the bathroom; I hear the light click on, and while the water's running I hear her gasp. "Eliora Monroe! What the fuck did you do to my neck?" she whisper-yells.

I smile to myself. "You told me to stay quiet."

"I meant bite your lip! Not make my neck look like I was attacked by leeches!" she exclaims, pointing at the side of her neck, which is indeed covered in at least three different hickeys.

"They'll probably fade by the morning!" I shrug, even though I know it's pretty unlikely that will happen.

Jax grumbles to herself, heads back to the bathroom, and comes back a minute later with some water. I sip it and place the rest on the nightstand.

"Is there any way I can make it up to you?" I say, batting my eyelashes at her.

"Oh, don't you start." She rolls her eyes.

"Please, Miss Evans. I don't want you to be angry with me."

"Mmm, maybe there is something you can do." She smirks.

"Get undressed and get on the bed," I command.

Jax strips out of her pajamas in record time and tosses them aside. She stands before me completely bare. Her pussy glistens with wetness and she has a cute little landing strip. Jax lies down in the middle of the bed, and I stand up at the end to take in all of her. She groans as she lies on the bed, exposed for me to see all of her. I bite my bottom lip—God, the way she whimpers is enough to make me clench my thighs together.

"What if you scissor me?" she suggests.

"You want to?"

"I want to," she nods, so I climb on top of her, one leg between her thighs and the other on the side of her hips.

Bending down, I kiss her again. This time with more passion. I want her, and I need her to know just how much. My hands roam her body, stopping at her delicate breasts and lingering at her nipples. I take her nipple in my mouth, and she whimpers softly. It is a beautiful sound.

"Oh, baby," she murmurs quietly.

"Don't forget to be quiet," I whisper, looking up at her from her chest.

I slide my hands around her chest, taking a moment to touch every inch of her before my hand finds her core. She's actually dripping for me, something I will never get tired of seeing or feeling. I want to taste her, but this isn't the time. She wants to scissor, and fuck if I would turn that down. I'm pretty sure there's no position she could recommend that I'd turn down. I slide my fingers up and down her core a few times, wetting her clit and covering my fingers in her juices. Then I look directly at Jax and suck my fingers clean. Her eyes widen as I lick them all over until they have no remnants of her.

"Fuck me already, naughty girl, please," she begs.

Positioning my pussy over hers, I hold her leg in the air and begin to rock my hips against hers. The second our swollen clits touch, we both let out a silent moan. Our lips make an O as we hold back the sounds. I hold her strong, muscular thighs in place while I ride on top of her. Jax is shaking her hips, too, meeting each motion with her own. If I hadn't just finished, I'd be coming in seconds. There's something about this position that always gets me off faster.

I look down at Jax, whose hands are gripping her breasts, playing with her nipples, and she's biting down on her bottom lip. I can see the imprint of her teeth in her lip; I'm worried she's going to make herself bleed.

"Fuck me, baby," Jax whimpers out. "Oh, I'm so close."

"Shhh!" I warn her. I don't know how serious it is to be quiet, but I don't want to ruin a moment like this.

Jax grips my hand, and we intertwine fingers as our hips rock against each other's. Rocking and bucking as our swollen clits beg for a release. Jax is closer than I am, and I want to get her there. I keep my hips moving, but I spit between us. Jax gasps as it hits our clits and fuels our rocking.

"Oh, El—" she starts to call out, but I put my hand over her mouth. It doesn't silence her until I put a few fingers in her mouth. She's biting on them, but it's not that hard, and I'd do anything to keep watching her orgasm.

"Fuck." Jax smiles at me while I collapse next to her. Jax might be the hottest woman I've ever been with, but there's no competition when it comes to her orgasms. Her face is one thing, but, fuck, the sounds and movements she makes are hot as hell.

After a few minutes Jax turns to me. "You didn't …"

I shake my head.

"Perfect," she says mischievously. She crawls to the edge of the bed, gets on her knees, and pulls my pussy to her face.

"Oh, Jax, you don't have to … Oh!" I stop myself when she presses her tongue to my clit.

"I know I don't have to, but I want to," she smiles. Not waiting for a reply, she drives her tongue back between my folds.

It's like she's attempting to sop up as much of my wetness as she possibly can. She whimpers under me, which makes me bite down on my lips. I'm trying hard to suppress my moans as much as I can. But Jax keeps whimpering and moaning against my pussy. You think it's hot to watch someone eat you out? It's even hotter when you can tell how much they're enjoying themselves. Jax acts like a starving animal having her first meal in weeks, and my pussy is reacting the same. I'm soaking her face and getting achingly close to finishing all over her.

"I'm close!" I gasp as quietly as I can.

"Don't come yet," she says, pausing.

"W-what?" I stare down at her.

"I'm not done with you yet." Her eyes are dark with desire as she whispers back to me.

I can only let out a quiet whimper as she swirls her tongue around my clit. I can feel my body dying for a release, and I'm doing everything I can to control myself. But there isn't much I can do when she's making it feel this fucking good. I can see her ass in the air, her dark curls peeking out over the swells of my stomach. Her tongue feels like heaven as she hums against me.

I can feel my heart beating out of my chest. I can't even reach for my nipples because my hands are so tightly gripping the sheets to keep me quiet. My thighs clench around Jax's face, and she only moans more. I slide my legs over her shoulders and tilt my hips back, something about this position making it even hotter. Maybe it's just knowing Jax is between my thighs and my ankles are literally dangling by her ears.

"Come for me," she finally commands, and I have to bite down on my own hand to suppress my moans.

Juices come squirting out of me, and Jax's face is soaked as she tries to catch it in her mouth. My eyes clamp shut as I try to watch, but the intensity is too powerful. I'm probably making a huge mess, but I don't even care. All I want is Jax and this moment of ecstasy.

Jax finally disappears from between my legs and returns with a warm washcloth. She rubs it all over the inside of my thighs, my pussy, and my stomach. She does it with this soft and gentle touch I didn't know she had. I feel like I'm a baby bird being taken care of for the first time. Is this why people say they cry during sex?

All I wanted was something to take my mind off this horrific day, and Jax managed to do that until now. I can't tell her that my father forbid me from seeing her. Or that I got into a fight about it with my sister. I don't want to argue about the best place for Mistletoe, or anything like that. I just wanted to come here and take my mind off everything.

"So, I can either change the sheets, or we can put a towel down, and I'll deal with that in the morning," Jax says softly, and I sit up to look at the huge wet spot I made.

I blush, my cheeks burning with embarrassment. "I'm so—"

"What did we say about that? I'm more than happy to clean up the mess. I just want to know what will make you most comfortable," Jax says, ignoring my apology.

"A towel is fine," I say.

"Towel it is." She disappears into the bathroom and returns with a dark, oversized towel. "In theory I should've put this down first, but it's not like I was planning to make you squirt."

"Weren't you?" I raise an eyebrow.

"Well, it's always on my mind. But whatever your body wants to do is cool with me," she laughs.

I glance at the TV and realize the movie is still on. It's on the credits, playing a holiday song as Jax and I get settled for bed. I put back on the pajamas, and Jax grabs a fresh set for herself. I thought it would feel sort of weird wearing her dead mom's pajamas, but I actually think it's kind of sweet. Jax kept them around, I'm sure for nostalgic reasons, and they are comfortable. I didn't know how she'd react seeing me in them, but it doesn't seem to be crossing her mind.

"How old were you when your mom died?" I ask.

"Uh, I was four, actually," Jax says quietly. That makes sense.

"Do you remember anything about her?"

"Not really. I remember the way she smelled, and certain things remind me of her, but I don't have too many memories of her or my dad. They were in the same car when they died," she explains.

"Oh my gosh, I don't realize." Now I feel like an asshole for bringing it up.

"It's okay. I don't mind talking about them; there aren't too many chances to talk about them with people who aren't my grandma. Everyone assumes I'm sad, and yeah, it is, but I also like to talk about their lives." She smiles.

"That's sweet. I've only lost extended family, so I just assumed it would be sad, but I like that a lot." I smile. "Does your grandma feel the same?"

"Most of the time. Sometimes she has times where she's sad or doesn't want to talk about it. So then we don't, but most of the time we're able to celebrate them for who they are."

I reach over and place my hand on Jax's chest just over her

heart. She's wearing a shirt, and it's not some boob grab; I just feel like I want to be closer to her. She puts her own hand on top of mine and smiles at me.

Jax

When I wake in the morning, there's a brief few seconds where I forget where I am. Except El's leg is wrapped around my waist, and I can smell her lavender perfume in her hair. My eyes flutter back closed until I see the light peeking in from the window. It isn't usually that bright when I get up in the morning. Oh shit, did I forget to set my alarm last night? El and I haven't even talked about today being Monday. We both have jobs that we seemed to forget about overnight. Not that I blame us. I pick up my phone and realize it's after nine in the morning. I don't know what time El has to be at work, but I assume it's earlier than this.

I nudge her softly, my palm on her shoulder, but she doesn't move. So I whisper her name and try again. This time she stirs and looks at me with one eye. "What's going on?" she grumbles.

"It's after nine; do you have to be at work or anything?" I ask.

"No, I'm working from home. I have a virtual meeting at three, but that's all," she explains, and then closes her eyes again.

If I don't go to the bookstore, there will be no one to open for Andrea later. And we really can't afford not to have someone there for the day. I don't want to bother El and wake her up, but

I don't know what else to do. Until I hear the clinking around of my grandma in the kitchen. I know she's been avoiding it, but if I can convince her to go in today, she'll be able to watch the store until later. I get dressed in pajamas and head downstairs to feel it out.

"Oh!" My grandma clutches her chest when she sees me. "I thought you were already gone."

"I'm actually hoping you can take my shift today. I, uh, don't feel okay and need someone to open up for Andrea," I explain.

"You're not feeling okay?" She stops to put a hand on her hip.

"Yeah."

"You must've been up late with that Monroe girl if you're not feeling so good." She smirks as my jaw drops.

"W-what?" I stutter.

"Oh, don't think you've got me fooled. I hear things, you know. I may be old, but people still like to tell me the gossip and news." She winks. "Plus, with those hickeys on your neck, I should hope she's here."

"Wait, you know that she's here?" I ask as I cover my neck.

"Yeah, I suspected when I saw your car in the driveway. You work hard, so I've called Andrea, and she's already stopped by for the key and is opening up. So if you'd like to 'be sick' a little longer, go for it." She laughs.

"I just thought you'd be more upset." I frown. This whole thing is throwing me off. Maybe I'm still sleeping and this is just a dream.

"Because you're having sex? You're an adult, do what—"

"Oh my God, no!" I cut her off. I'll have to scrub my ears clean. "Because it's a Monroe."

"I'm not thrilled about it, but you can't choose who you love." My grandma shrugs.

"Oh, it's not—"

"Mmm, keep telling yourself that." She winks at me.

"Hey, I hope I'm not interrupting anything." El peeks around the corner of the kitchen wall. How long has she been there? How much does she hear?

"You must be the infamous El." My grandma smiles.

"I'm Eliora, but everyone calls me El." She reaches out to shake my grandma's hand.

"I'm Ms. Evans, but everyone calls me Grandma." She winks.

"I'm sorry for intruding. I was looking for Mistletoe and heard Jax down here," El says.

"Mistletoe?" My grandma looks between us, confused.

"It's our cat," I say, realizing that doesn't explain it any better.

"We found a cat in the snow with a hurt paw and no tags. It doesn't seem to have any owners, so we've been taking care of it," El explains.

"That's so sweet, and she's here somewhere?" my grandma asks.

"Yes, she was upstairs with us, and now she seems to be wandering about," El says.

"She can't get too far; I'm sure if we put out some of her food, she'd come running," I say.

As if on cue, Mistletoe comes sauntering through the kitchen. She stops to look at my grandma before rubbing her body against the backs of her legs. She circles her a few times before lying at her feet.

"She must like you." I smile.

"I thought I heard a creature sauntering around. I was worried we had a possum or something." Grandma laughs.

"Do you want to stay for breakfast, El?" Grandma asks.

"Oh, I don't want to impose."

"It's no trouble. I always make way too much food as is." My grandma smiles.

"Okay, then sure. I'll just go get... changed." El looks at me and then heads upstairs.

"You couldn't have been any quieter?!" I growl at my grandma quietly.

"It's not like she doesn't feel the same!" My grandma shrugs.

I ignore her. She's spent less than five minutes with her; how could she possibly know that? When I get upstairs, El is in the middle of putting on clean clothes.

"Your grandma invited me for breakfast!? Should I be worried it's poisoned?" she whispers at me.

"No!" I shake my head. "I don't know what's up with her, but she's not like that."

"Am I to believe our family's rivalry could've been solved with someone offering the other breakfast?" El says sarcastically.

"No, but I don't think the issue she has is with you specifically," I say carefully.

"Ah, that makes more sense then." She nods.

"Come down for breakfast, and then maybe after we can talk? I know you didn't want to last night, but I think maybe we can today." I suggest. I'm nervous about what might come of that, but it's better we communicate like adults instead of dancing around it.

"Yeah, we can," she agrees.

We head downstairs together, and my grandma is setting up plates of food for us at the table. Full of pancakes, bacon, and eggs. It's way too much food for anyone to eat, but that is how my grandma does things.

"So, I can assume how y'all met, right?" My grandma, ever the icebreaker.

"Uh, yeah, I'm helping my dad out by looking over the contracts he has with the bookstore. I am sorry about that; I'm just helping out my family. I don't even practice law here; I'm a real estate attorney in the city," El explains nervously.

"It's you who got us evicted?" That feels like a hard punch to the gut. I always thought she happened to be in town and did the favor of delivering, not that she is the one who set it into motion.

"Technically, yes." She sighs and looks at me with eyes full of regret. Or maybe that is just wishful thinking. "My father asked me to look things over, and I only mentioned it as a technicality. I think it's a last-minute resort. He is so pressed to find a solution to make my grandfather happy."

"Ah, old Jamie is just as heartbroken as he's ever been, isn't he?" My grandma shakes her head.

"You know my grandfather? I mean, like more than just business-wise?" El asks. My curiosity is piqued, too, at her heartbroken comment.

"Eh, it's about time I just tell you the story." My grandma shrugs. "Your grandfather, Jamie, asked me out many, many years ago. I turned him down—I just never saw him in that way —and he didn't handle it well. I suppose he might've handled it better had I not gone out with his best friend."

"Who was his best friend?" I ask, confused. As far as I know, my grandma only dated my grandfather.

"Your grandfather. You know he was my one and only." My grandma smiles.

"Oh my God. So my grandpa has been trying to get revenge for the last fifty years because you married his best friend and rejected him?!" El gasps.

"I suppose so. We tried talking to him when Robert, my husband, was alive, but he wasn't interested. He saw it as a betrayal and never let go. When we bought the bookstore, he vowed to try and take it from us. We've been fighting off his evictions for as long as I can remember." Grandma sighs.

I don't know what to say. I have about a million choice words right now, but it is El's grandfather, so I'm trying to be sensitive about that.

"Well, just tell me he's the world's smallest man without telling me he's the smallest. Like, damn, Grandpa—he's married and has kids and grandkids. How the hell is he not over someone he didn't even go out with?! That's insane. And no way does my family know any of this. We're all under the impression this is about property!" El exclaims.

My grandma starts laughing. "I like her."

I glance at the spitfire woman I've come to know, and I can't help but agree. El is passionate, and even when she is wrong, she doesn't stand down if it's what she believes in. She looks as stunned as I feel to find out the truth about our families. Who knew it was all about a little best-friend rivalry and my grandma being a baddie back in the day.

"I'm so sorry for my family's stupidity. I have to hope my father doesn't know the actual reason, or he wouldn't be so hard-pressed to have you guys out." El sighs.

"Is there anything you can do?" I ask. Up until now, I've avoided talking about the bookstore with her, but maybe she's seeing things in a new light.

"No, I honestly wish I could, but once the eviction notice is up there's nothing to do. It either needs to be paid, or my father could rescind it. But even knowing this, I'm not one hundred percent sure he would do that." She frowns.

"Oh." That is a letdown.

"I'm sorry. I really wish I never have any part in this. There's so much I wish I could do now." El looks at me solemnly.

"It's not your fault. I've been telling Jax the same thing. It was a long time coming, and it'll all work out the way it needs to. I'm not afraid of any Monroes, and I don't blame you for helping your family. I'm sure if roles were reversed, Jax would do the same for me." My grandma pats El's hand.

I open my mouth to protest, but I stop when I realize she's right. If my grandma had a good reason, asked me for help in my job field, and said it is important, of course I wouldn't hesitate to help. That's just the kind of thing you do for family. It's not like she ever holds a grudge with me, even when I make it easier for her to.

"Breakfast is lovely, but I actually have to get back to the city if I want to make my meeting on time, unless I do the meeting here. But I don't think I have the notes I need. " El says, looking at her watch.

"You're taking the train?" I ask.

"Yeah, if you don't mind giving me a ride?" She smiles.

"Of course." I nod, grabbing the breakfast plates and placing them in the sink. I will take care of them later.

"Thank you again for having me, Ms. Evans. I appreciate it." El smiles at my grandma, who shocks me by pulling her in for a hug.

"Come back anytime," she says, just loud enough for me to hear.

El grabs her things, and I follow her upstairs. We still haven't talked about Mistletoe.

"I think she should stay here. Your grandma seems to like her, and there's more room. Plus, I'm kind of hoping it gives me a good excuse to come visit?" El says sheepishly.

"Are you sure? I realize the city isn't exactly as dirty and smelly as I thought it was."

"I'm sure." She nods.

El says goodbye to our cat, and I take her bag to the car. It is a short ride into town, and the train is scheduled to come soon.

"I have this work thing this week; I thought maybe you'd want to come. If you're not too busy or anything," El says nonchalantly. But I can tell this is important to her.

"You want me to come with you?" I look at El, who is currently avoiding eye contact.

"I mean, only if you want to. It's a work thing, so it won't be fun, but I get to dress up, and there's an open bar." She smiles.

"Why didn't you say that? Open bar is fun." I chuckle.

"You're not worried about what people might say? Or think?" she asks quietly.

"Am I worried a room full of strangers might see me with a beautiful woman and be jealous? Oh, absolutely. But I'm not worried about much else." I smirk.

"You know that's not what I mean." She stares at me.

"We already told my grandma and she loves you. So why would I care what anyone else thinks?"

"I don't know." She pauses. "My father told me to stay away

from you. He actually said I'd be betraying the family if I'm with you."

"Oh. That's crazy," I say. "Is that why you were so upset last night?"

"Yes, I'm fighting with him, and then I was at my sister's, and she argued with me about it too. She thinks I'm stupid for wanting to end this because of him, but I don't even know if there is a *this* to end," El explains.

"Is that what you want?" I ask.

"No. I wish my father would understand, and maybe if I tell him the truth about Grandpa, he'll come around. But either way, I'm not going to let him tell me who I can be with." El smiles.

"So tell me, is this event black tie, or do I just need a really fancy button-down?" I tease, changing the subject just a bit. I can tell El needs a change, and now that I know where we stand, I don't mind.

"It's not that fancy, but I am wearing a cocktail dress. It's our holiday party, so maybe something red or green?" She smiles, her red lipstick making her lips look even bigger.

"Well, there go my plans of wearing a Santa suit. Right out the window!" I chuckle, and El laughs.

"Someone did that last year and was drunk an hour later— and tried to sit on everyone else's laps. So please don't do that," El says.

NINETEEN

El

I'm sitting at my vanity attempting to put on mascara when Jax kisses the side of my neck. She pulls my hair to one side and places her puckered lips on the nape of my neck. I can see her smirking in the mirror as she does it too. She's way too pleased with herself. I put my mascara down and look at her. She kept her promise and is wearing a dark green sweater instead of the Santa suit she joked about.

"How am I supposed to get ready if you keep doing that?" I groan.

"Well, maybe you should stop." She wiggles her eyebrows seductively.

"We don't have time for that."

"What if we make time?" She takes my hand, pulling me up to stand.

My body presses against hers, and she smiles at me. The corners of my lips betray me as I smile back at her. Jax takes that as an invitation to kiss me, and she's probably smudging the red lipstick I just put on, but the kiss is worth it. I can feel it all the way in my toes as her tongue slides against mine. Her hard body leans against the softness of my own as she helps me stand. I wrap my arms around her neck while she kisses me. We might not have time to do it, but we definitely have time for this.

Whenever Jax kisses me, I feel this electricity coursing through my veins. It's this power she has, like she's awakening me when I didn't even know I'd been sleeping. The palms of her hands rest on my hips, and I can feel her chest heaving gently against mine. I tangle my hands in the curls of her hair, and she nibbles on my bottom lip. God, I could get lost in kissing her; it's like nothing else in the world even matters. Jax moans lightly as her tongue swipes across my lips, and I grip her hair tighter. She slides her hands around the sides of my hips and grabs my ass.

I'm not dressed yet, still in my leggings and a loose T-shirt, so she grips my ass tightly. I can feel the imprint of both her hands making their mark on my ass. I groan against her body as she pulls me in closer. She's going to make me late, but I don't care. I can't, not with the way she's touching me.

"El?!" Pulling away from Jax, I feel like I've been electrocuted.

Standing before Jax and me is my ex-girlfriend, Tara. Dressed in a deep red floor-length gown, her hair done and makeup ready, I stare at her in confusion.

"Tara? What are you doing here?" I shake my head, trying to recall if I'm missing some key information, all while Jax holds my hand and looks stunned.

"It's your office's holiday party; we go every year," Tara says like it's obvious.

"When we're together, yes. But we're not together anymore."

"Well, that's obvious by how quickly you've moved on."

"Maybe I should go…" Jax starts.

"Maybe you should," Tara says sassily, rolling her eyes.

"No, I promise this is just a misunderstanding," I say to Jax, reaching for her hand. "Tara, you need to go. I don't know why you even still have a key to this place."

"Because I live here with you. And maybe that doesn't mean much to you anymore, but it means more to me," Tara says.

"I'm not saying it doesn't mean anything, but you can't just pop in anytime you'd like," I say angrily.

"Don't worry, I checked the cameras. I thought you were alone; I guess I didn't check carefully enough. Whoops."

"The cameras?" Jax says anxiously.

"She didn't tell you? The Ring camera in the front door. I texted her about it last week; she of course mostly ignored me. But I caught a nice video of the two of you spending the weekend together," Tara says smugly.

"I think I should go." Jax grabs her jacket and starts to storm out.

"Jax!" I run after her. "Wait!"

"What?" She turns around, her face full of hurt and fury.

"It's not what it sounds like," I plead.

"It sounds like your ex texted you and you didn't think to mention it. It also sounds like your ex is able to walk into your apartment whenever they want, and you're maybe not as broken up as you claim," Jax exclaims.

"I swear, we started as a break, but we're broken up. She moved out weeks ago, and there's nothing else between us," I tell her.

"I just can't do this. I can't be in the middle of this much drama right now. I should be focusing on getting my bookstore handled. It's not like you've been a big help in that," Jax snaps.

I pull back. Her words hit like ice on my skin. I didn't know she was still upset with me about my involvement in the eviction. It isn't like I knew her when I set the whole thing up. All I did was offer my father some off-the-books legal advice. He is a businessman, and I thought I was helping. I thought I'd be putting an old feud behind us once and for all. But apparently, I was wrong.

"I just need some time." Jax leaves out the front door.

For a second, I almost let her go. But something makes me call after her, makes me chase down that freaking elevator, just for a chance at talking to her. The elevator doors are closed before I get there, and any remnants of her are gone. I sulk back to my apartment and slam the door for good measure.

"I wasn't sure you were coming back." Tara smiles as she lounges on our couch. Well, it's mine now, after all.

"Tara, what the hell are you doing here?" I say angrily.

"I think we're going to the party together." She frowns.

"You have to be on drugs to think that we've broken up but are still going to this together. So now tell me why you're really here." I cross my arms and look at her.

"I just think maybe we can talk about this. It all happened so abruptly, and I thought maybe if I showed up, you and I could talk," she admits with a shaky voice.

"I don't know what there is to talk about." I sigh.

"We've taken breaks before, but it never felt like this. I thought it was going to be like all the other times where we spent a few weeks apart and then got back together," Tara explains.

"Did you think maybe I don't want that anymore?"

"What do you mean?" she asks.

"We're adults. If it was meant to be, do you think we would've had to spend so much time apart?" I ask.

"Is that how you feel? Or is that what you're saying because you've clearly met someone else?" She scoffs.

"I thought I wanted this to work because we've put so much time and effort into it, but the truth is I don't think I love you in the way I want to feel about my person. You're amazing, but the way we fight and spend so much time apart isn't what I want anymore. We don't make each other happy anymore, and I think it's time we break up for good," I say.

"Are you serious?" Tara's jaw drops.

"I am. It's something I've been thinking about. And no, it doesn't have anything to do with anyone else. I just don't want to spend the rest of my life fighting for the passion I can feel naturally with someone," I explain.

"Wow." I've left Tara speechless.

"I know this isn't what you were looking for. And I'm sorry; I do care about you. I just think we should end it."

"Fine. I guess it's not like you've left me with much of a choice." She stands and looks around.

"Is there anything you need? I will be removing you from the Ring account too," I tell her.

"No, I took what I needed when I moved out." She shrugs.

"I'm sorry this is how things turned out; I do care about you." It's not a lie.

I spent the last several years with Tara, and despite our differences, I do love her. I just know I don't love her in the way I feel about Jax. The way that Jax lights me up and makes me feel things for her I didn't know are possible. Until I met her, I thought what Tara and I had was normal. I thought that was how I was supposed to feel about people I love. Now I'm seeing things entirely different.

"I hope you can get her back." Tara kisses my cheek and heads out the door.

I lock the door behind her and take a moment to gather my thoughts. All I want to do is track down Jax and tell her this is all a big misunderstanding. But I also know she's still holding on to how I'm part of the bookstore's downfall. And it seems like something we might not be able to move past. It's her family's legacy, and I helped destroy it like it was nothing. I should know better than to listen to my father.

I glance at the clock, realizing I still need to get to the party. I head back to my room, quickly finish my makeup, and throw on the new dress I bought. I've been looking forward to surprising Jax with it. It's red, down to my knees with a slit up the side, and shows off my ample chest proudly. Now I'm arriving late to my boss's party without a buffer. If it wasn't so late, I might have called Bells to save me. But this is something I have to face on my own.

"Miss Monroe! You look breathtaking!" My bosses are two gay men who founded the practice twenty years ago. They've been married for almost forty years, and the practice is their child.

"Thank you, Seth and Blake. You both look fabulous as usual." I smile. They greet me with a kiss on each cheek, and a waiter hands me a glass of champagne.

"No one with you tonight? I thought you mentioned bringing someone," Seth asks.

"They couldn't make it—last-minute family emergency," I lie.

"Understandable. Do you need to go too?" Blake asks.

"Nope, they insisted I come tonight." They look at me skeptically but don't push the issue.

I check my coat and head for the open bar. I've already finished two glasses of champagne, and I want to drink this night away. I'm sipping a vodka tonic when I feel someone tap my shoulder.

"Oh, Leah, you look lovely. Did you bring someone tonight?" I ask my assistant as I greet her with a hug.

"I did. El, this is my wife, Gabriella." Leah introduces me to a short brunette with huge curly hair and tan skin. She ironically looks a lot like Gabby from Desperate Housewives.

"Wow! I didn't know you were married; it's so nice to meet you, Gabriella." I smile and shake Leah's wife's hand.

"It's great to meet you. Leah talks a lot about work, and you're always spoken of in such a positive light. It's nice to meet someone she speaks of so fondly," Gabriella smiles.

"You talk about me at home?" I gasp, clutching my chest. "I'm so flattered."

"You're one of the best bosses I've ever had." Leah blushes.

"It's true; I don't think she's complained about you once," Gabriella teases.

"Are you back in the office after the holidays? It hasn't been the same without you there," Leah asks.

I've always been able to work in a hybrid format. It's something I worked into my contract when I started. I like having the option to work from home or the office or anywhere in between. But I've been using most of my time lately to work from home. I'm still up to date with everything, but it's weird not going into work most mornings. I've been spending more time than I anticipated in Evergreen Valley and less time at my own place.

"I should be, yes," I assure her.

"Thank goodness. We'll let you mingle—have a good night." Leah and Gabby excuse themselves, and I knock back the rest of my drink.

I spend the rest of the night being polite to the firm's partners and saying hello to people I only see once a year. I don't dance or pay attention to the music, but I do hit up the open bar as much as I can. With shaky hands and blurry vision, I reach for my phone in my purse. It takes three tries for me to unlock it, but then I'm in, and I'm looking through my recently called list. Why does drinking make everything so blurry? I close one eye to steady my sight, but I can only see my eyelashes instead. I click call and put the phone up to my ear. It rings and rings for what feels like forever. Don't calls have to go to voicemail at some point?

When it's time to leave a voicemail, I drunkenly tell Jax how much I miss her and how I wish she was here with me tonight. I tell her things are over with Tara and how much of a misunderstanding it all was. I'm in the middle of a sentence when the voicemail beeps at me, and I grumble, hanging up. I don't know if she'll call me back tonight, but I keep my ringer on just in case. Deciding that I've been here long enough, I decide to grab a cab home. There's no way I can make it back on the train with all the snow and these shaky legs. I can walk in heels when I'm sober, but right now it's killing me not to take them off. I'm about one minute away from kicking them off and running through the snow to numb my hurting feet.

Thankfully, a taxi pulls up, and I tell them my address. I text Bells where I am so at least someone knows what I'm up to. By the time I'm climbing into bed, I completely forget about taking off my shoes. I plop face down into the bed and inhale Jax's scent on my sheets. Pine and peppermint fills my nostrils, and I close my eyes, drifting easily to sleep as I imagine Jax beside me. I'll probably feel like shit in the morning, but at least for now I'm in bed.

TWENTY

Jax

______

The worst part about storming off on someone who lives in a different town is not being able to go anywhere. I have to stand on the cold street for fifteen minutes until an actual yellow cab comes along. For the life of me I can't recall which train El and I usually take. And it isn't like I'm going to call her up and ask. I grumble all the way to Grand Central and get myself on the first train back to Evergreen Valley. I only stop to get my car from the train station and then drive straight to Parker's house. It's nighttime, but only after eight, so Parker is still awake.

"Do you need wine or vodka?" Parker asks after she opens the door for me.

"Vodka," I say, making my way inside.

"I had a feeling, considering this is the last place you should be right now."

"It's the only place I want to be right now," I grumble as I take a seat on her couch.

"You going to tell me what happened?" Parker asks. She places two glasses on the coffee table, pours a shot of vodka in each, and hands me one. I down it instantly.

"Her ex showed up at their apartment—the one she only

recently moved out of—and it seems like things aren't as over as El made them out to be," I say, taking a second shot.

"I thought she said she was single?" Parker asks.

"Apparently, they split not too long ago. So the ex showed up ready to go to the party tonight and tried kicking me out. But then I felt awkward, so I kicked myself out," I sigh.

"Why?"

"What do you mean, why? Because she had another woman over. And because she's the woman responsible for destroying my grandmother's legacy. She helped her father figure out how to get us evicted," I explain.

"I mean, that's shitty, but it's not like she knew you when she did it. She was helping out her family," Parker says.

I stare at her, my eyebrows crushing together. "How can you be on her side right now?"

"I'm not on her side; I'm just telling you I do understand."

"You understand what?"

"I'm not trying to fight with you. If you want me to just listen right now, I don't have to offer my opinion," Parker says, putting up her hands defensively.

"No, it's fine," I say.

"I can see why she'd be conflicted now because her family probably puts a lot of pressure on her. And I'm sure it wasn't her first choice to drive you guys to eviction. But she's a lawyer, right? So it's more like she's doing her job for the family. She isn't looking at you guys as people, but more as a client she has to check off her to-do list," Parker explains, and I hate how much she sounds right about this.

Thankfully, my phone rings and I'm saved by the bell. Except when I turn it over, I see El's photo illuminating the screen. It's a photo I took of her on our date ice skating. She looks so happy, skating around the rink without a care in the world. I can't bring myself to pick up right now. I'm too upset, and I have been drinking. I don't think it's a good idea to mix that right now. She leaves a voicemail, and I press the phone to my ear to listen to it.

"Hi, Jax…" She sounds drunk, slurring my name. "I'm so sorry about today. I miss you so much. I'm at my work party, and it's not the same without you here. I wish you were with me. I hope you'll call me back tomorrow or let me come see you. I don't want to fight or stress—what the heck? It didn't even let me leave a full message?! That's bullshit." She grumbles, and the line clicks off. She must have heard a beeping sound and thought it was the signal for the end of the answering machine.

I can't help but laugh. I save the message instead of deleting it, realizing that might be the last place I have a copy of her voice. Parker returns from the kitchen with a plate of pizza rolls and Bagel Bites—our signature drinking-night snack. I relax a bit, knowing El apologized and things are over with her ex. But I'm still hesitant to keep things going. My focus needs to be on keeping the bookstore from closing, and I don't need anything getting in the way of that.

"So, did you happen to see my neighbor on the way in?" Parker asks.

"The new one? No, but I think I saw a kid and a dog?" I try to remember, but I wasn't exactly taking the time to look around when I got here.

"That's them. My neighbor Tessa has two kids and a dog," she explains.

"Is this the hot single mom you've been flirting with?" I tease.

"Maybe." Parker laughs. "Yeah, she's kind of amazing, but it's been a hassle trying to convince her to let me take her out. I think her ex is a bit of a dick."

"We've all had one of those," I laugh.

"Jax? Can you help me put the paintings up?" Paige asks as we stand in the rec room of the library. We are putting the final touches on the place for the party and silent auction that is only a few days away.

A group of local artists has graciously donated paintings to be hung during the event. They are all holiday-themed and then will be auctioned off at the end of the night. I'm terribly hungover from my night with Parker, but I'm determined to get this done. I'm sucking down electrolytes and Tylenol like it's no one's business and working harder than anyone. Sure, maybe I threw up a few times earlier, but I brushed my teeth and moved on.

"Have you talked to El?" Paige asks, causing me to almost drop my side of the painting.

"No. Have you?" I avoid eye contact.

"No. She said she was coming, but it's been a few days since I've heard from her. Aren't you guys, like, seeing each other?" She looks at me, confused.

"Uh…" I don't know what to say. It's complicated.

"Got it. I just want to know if she's still coming to the event. We sort of had a fight, and I thought maybe I'd get the chance to apologize in person," Paige explains.

"I'm not sure," I admit.

I try to get Parker's attention from across the room, so she'll come save me from this awkwardness, but she's too distracted by her neighbor. Her neighbor is one of the new librarians, who has just started in the last few weeks. She has long dark hair and tattoos all over her arms. It's weird seeing a librarian who isn't old and knitting, but then again it isn't like Paige looks like that either. It seems we need to update our perception of librarians.

"Give El some time," Paige says.

"What?"

"She's still under my family's spell that things will all work out if she listens to them. It's a hard thing to break free from, but since she's been with you it's like she's finally seeing things clearly. So whatever is going on with you guys, just give her some time," Paige explains.

Before I can reply, she heads to the other side of the room to get another painting. We continue putting them up in silence while I think about what she said. I miss El; it has only been a day, and I already miss the way she smells and her laugh. I miss kissing her and how it feels waking up next to her. I don't want to do this event without seeing her by my side. But will her family even allow that? I know they don't want El and me to be together, but I don't know if El is ready to stand up to them yet. Paige and her are clearly on different sides of things, and I don't want to fight it.

My grandma is finally willing to be at the bookstore again. I don't know if she believes I can actually pull this off or if she's missing it. But either way, she is spending her mornings sitting behind the counter knitting instead of at home, which means she is in a much better mood all around when I get home. She even took care of Mistletoe for me when I was at Parker's last night.

This event is coming together. Once we have all the decorations up, the janitors come in to put the tables and chairs up. There will be room for dancing, but also tables and chairs for everyone to sit and enjoy the night. We have a local college kid DJing the event with the promise he can livestream it. I figure the more publicity the better, and we have a makeshift stage on one end. It allows people to make speeches and announce the auction winners. Once we hit the goal, I'll prepare a few words and thank everyone for their generosity and support.

To say I'm nervous is an understatement. I have everything riding on this event, and if it falls through, I don't know what I'll do. I think if the funding falls through, I don't know if El and I can make it through. Not that I know for sure there even is an El and me anymore. But knowing her family is the reason behind my family's eviction, I don't know how we can get past that. So everything feels a little heavier than it did before. I have the two most important things in my life, besides my grandma, riding on this event going well and getting the funding.

The next two days go by in a blur. Everyone is asking me a

million questions, and I'm just trying to get through it as quickly as possible. I check over my to-do list three times and make sure everything is done. Even if someone tells me it's done, I have to check it myself because I'm that paranoid. I probably get less than five hours of sleep, but I'll sleep next week. Right now, all that matters is pulling this off.

Paige and Parker are my best helpers. They're the ones who send me home the day of the event to get some sleep. They promise to call me if for some reason my alarm doesn't go off and I'm not here early to check everything again. When I do get home, my sheets still smell like El. I'm careful not to sleep on her side of the bed so as not to disturb the smell. I'm savoring it, like a kid with his last cookie. I don't know if she'll be in my bed again, and I don't want to lose this feeling.

I get my outfit for the night together on my closet door and check once more that my alarm for this nap is set. My grandma isn't home, but I have a feeling she's at the bookstore again. Andrea has been keeping her busy by making TikToks together —which is exactly as hilarious as it sounds. Andrea finds the trending sounds, makes them book-related, and has my grandma act them out. She started an account for us, and while it only has a hundred followers, I can see it growing. I'm just happy to see my grandma doing something that makes her happy.

By the time my head hits the pillow, I'm passed out.

TWENTY-ONE

El

___

I show up at the train station and see Paige waiting for me. She's standing outside her car, leaning against it with an unreadable face. We haven't seen each other in person since our fight, and we've only started texting again this morning. I was willing to take a cab, but I figured I should mend fences with Paige. It is a day of hopefully getting people in Evergreen Valley to forgive me. As I walk closer to her, she smiles, and I feel more relaxed than I have in days.

"I'm sorry for our fight," I say as she hugs me. She squeezes me even tighter, and I laugh.

"I know, I'm sorry too. I just wish Mom and Dad didn't have you so tight under their thumb," she says as we get in the car.

"I think I'm finally seeing things for what they are," I admit. "Which is why I'm hoping you'll take me to their house first."

"Why?" She looks at me, confused.

"I want to see if they'll drop the eviction against Jax and her grandmother. Maybe if I try to explain it to them, or talk to them, they'll understand."

"You know this is Dad we're talking about, right?" She cracks a smile.

"I know. But I also found out some stuff that Dad might not

know. Like, yes, Grandpa Jamie asked out Jax's grandmother first, and she turns him down to marry his best friend. But Dad thinks Grandpa had first dibs on the bookstore, and that's not true; Jax's grandma is the one who was interested in it from the start. I think he's still holding a grudge, but maybe if I explain that to Dad, he might let go. I mean, it's been almost fifty years—isn't it time?" I explain.

"Damn, Grandpa can be stubborn." Paige shakes her head. "I'll drive you there, but I'm not coming in. I haven't talked to them since our last family dinner."

"Okay. Will you wait for me?" I ask hopefully.

"Of course. You might need a getaway car," she jokes.

We pull up to our parents' house, and somehow it feels more daunting than ever. Nothing's changed, the house looking just as clean and pristine as ever, but I feel as if I'm walking into a haunted house. Paige parks in the driveway and I knock on the door alone. I probably have the key to their place somewhere in my bag, but I don't want to walk in unannounced. They definitely prefer that we don't do that.

"Oh! Eliora, what a surprise!" My mother greets me with a kiss and invites me in. "Your father is in his office; I assume you're here to talk to him?"

"How'd you know?" I ask.

"It's a small town, dear; I just had a feeling." She smiles and leads me to his office, encouraging me to go in.

"Dad?" I ask, knocking and peeking through the open door.

"Come in," he says gruffly.

"I thought maybe we could discuss..." I start.

"Are you here to talk about how you're dating the Evans granddaughter? Because I thought you nipped that in the bud," he sighs.

"No, I'm here to talk about Grandpa and his stubbornness and grudge against the Evans," I say sternly. I know how this goes; I've been in plenty of meetings with older men who like to command the room. If I give him an inch, he'll take a mile. I need to be in charge here.

"Eliora, you're starting to sound like your sister," he sighs, taking off his glasses, placing them on his desk, and rubbing the bridge of his nose.

"Thank you; I take that as a compliment," I smile. "I understand you think Grandpa is humiliated and that's why he wants the property, but the truth is the property was never his to begin with."

"What? Who told you that? You can't believe everything an Evans tells you," he scoffs.

"Ms. Evans did tell me that, but I've done some research, and she was the first one to apply for a loan at the bank for the bookstore. Grandpa didn't even know about the property until her husband told him about it. He was jealous of them, that is true, but it is never about the building. It was about the woman," I explain.

"But he's a married man. It's been fifty years, and he has kids, grandkids—it's not like he hasn't moved on." My father tries to make sense of what I've said.

"I know. But it's the truth. I think he feels hurt because he not only lost the woman he had feelings for, but he also lost his best friend."

"So what are you asking here?" He seems to snap out of his confusion and go back to business.

"I want you to drop the eviction. The bookstore belongs to the Evans, and it's not up to us to kick them out. They're doing everything they can, and they should be rewarded for that."

"No way. It's already set in motion, and I'm not backing out of a deal that could change so much for us." He shakes his head.

"But what would it really change? We don't need another condo building or more money. But you're taking away a family's livelihood and a lot of readers' joy."

"You're only changing your mind on these things because you've been brainwashed by your girlfriend," he says.

"That's not true." I clench my fists. "I love our family, but I'm tired of being on the wrong side of things. If you don't drop the eviction notice, then I'll just help them pay off the debt myself."

"Not with a cent of Monroe money you won't. That's family money, and I can assure you it will be declined before you even finish writing the check," my father says angrily.

"You can't control my money," I snap.

"I can if it's Monroe money. You will not slap this family in the face by not only dating the grandchild of your enemy but also funding their stay!" my father stands as he yells.

I know it's useless to yell back, so I storm out. I slam the office door behind me as well as the front door. I don't say goodbye to my mother, and I make it back to Paige's car. She doesn't say anything when I get in and angrily put on my seat belt, which takes longer than necessary because nothing goes right when you're angry and I miss the click twice.

"I take it things don't go well?" she says as we get to her house.

"Dad isn't budging on anything, and he threatened me. He says I can't use my own money to help Jax. Which is crazy because he may give me some, but I do make my own," I say angrily.

"Why can't you just use your own then?" Paige asks.

"What?"

"Like, if you know how much is actually yours, why can't you just use that money? I'm sure you know your salary and paycheck, right? So only take that amount; that way, if it's questioned, you can prove it's yours," Paige explains.

"Oh my God, I could kiss you. That's perfect!" I start thinking about the math in my head. I definitely have enough to cover Jax's eviction notice.

"Do you think Jax will actually take it?" Paige asks.

"What do you mean?" I frown.

"She seems too proud to take a handout from someone. But

especially from you. Do you think she'll just take the money from you to pay Dad?" Paige says.

"Well, she can pay me back if she wants."

"It's not about that." Paige shakes her head. "I just feel like she wouldn't accept it from you if she didn't earn it."

"You're right," I sigh.

I wish there is a way I could get her to accept it without her knowing it's from me. But then again, that's not necessarily a secret I want to hold on to. It doesn't seem like a good way to start a new relationship. Not that we are necessarily starting one either. This whole situation is making my head spin.

"Why don't we focus on getting you ready? The party is in two hours, and you still look like you just stepped off the train," Paige says.

"Fine, fine. Do your worst," I joke.

Paige leads me inside and I take a quick shower, washing my hair and the smell of the train off me. Then I blow-dry my hair straight and tie it in a high ponytail. I have the perfect dress for tonight, something I had to order online after seeing it in the store earlier this week. I was worried it wouldn't come in time, but just before I left the delivery came and it fits like a glove. The red dress has tulle sleeves, a V-neck top, and glitter all over the dress. But the shoes are what make it. They are red with white fur on the top and a small yellow bell on the front. The bell doesn't jingle, but it's still just as cute.

"I need to do my hair; are you done yet?" Paige asks, shoving her way into her very small bathroom.

"I guess so," I laugh. "I'll do my makeup in your room."

"Good." Paige shuts the door behind me, and I sit on her bed.

Spreading out all my makeup, I use my phone as a mirror. I see Paige's roommates walk by since the bedroom door is open, and they all take turns saying hello. Paige has convinced them to come tonight so there will be a bigger turnout. She says Jax is really worried about it and doesn't know how many people will actually show up.

"Hello?" Bells picks up on the second ring.

"I need a favor," I say, not missing a beat.

"What's up?" Bells chews something crunchy as she asks.

"Tonight is Jax's gala to avoid eviction, and we're worried about the final head count. Do you think you and Tilly can drive over? I know it's last minute."

"Of course. Tilly has snow tires and I'm always down for a party. Shoot me an address and we'll be there as soon as I get dressed," Bells says happily.

"Thank you! Oh my goodness, I love you." I hang up and send Bells the address.

BELLS: Might have to convince Tills if you know what I mean 😜

ME: get it girl!

"Is Bells coming?" Paige asks, walking into her room.

"Yeah, how'd you know?"

"She's your best friend. I figure if you asked, she'd definitely make it. A few extra people will make Jax feel better." Paige smiles.

"I just hope I'll get a chance to talk to her." I sigh.

I tried talking to her before tonight, but either her phone is off or she's ignoring me. All my calls go to voicemail, and she hasn't called me back or anything. Not that I thought she'd respond to my drunk call. I sort of hope she doesn't even listen to the voicemail because I can't even remember what I said. I think maybe we'll get the chance tonight to talk things out, but I don't want to put too much pressure on her either. I know most of her focus will be on raising the money for tonight.

Maybe I can have Bells write the check? No. I'm sure Jax won't want to take it from someone who's basically a stranger if she won't take it from me. And she definitely won't take it from my best friend. That would be like me taking money from Parker. I could try to do an anonymous donation, but I'm sure in a small town like this it would take only seconds for someone to figure it out. Maybe I have to bid on all the baskets and win all of them? But no, I'm sure that would just piss Jax off, and then I'd be stuck with a million Evergreen Valley things to do without the one person who keeps me here.

"What do you think of this?" Paige holds up a dress in one hand and a jumper in the other.

"I like the jumper; the color suits your skin tone," I tell her.

"Perfect." She nods.

"Is your boyfriend coming tonight?" I ask nosily.

"He's not my boyfriend. And no, he's out of town with his family this week," she explains.

"Oh, that sucks. He won't even be here for Christmas?" I ask.

"Nope. But it's fine; we're really not anything serious," she shrugs.

"Paige? Do you have any shoes I can borrow? I don't seem to have anything that goes with my outfit," Sierra asks.

"Uh, let me see." Paige jumps over to her closets and begins rummaging through the bottom. A pile of shoes turns into a scavenger hunt, so I turn back to finishing my makeup.

Glancing at the time, I suddenly feel my nerves piling up. I'm going to see Jax again for the first time in days. But it's also the fact that I'm going to tell Jax how much she means to me. I haven't admitted it out loud, as it's terrifying to think about, but I know how I feel. Jax is something special and not something I'm willing to let go of. I just hope she feels the same.

A few days ago, I wouldn't have hesitated with this. I would have just told her how I felt and know we are on the same page. But now I'm worried I'm about to make a fool of myself. I know her feelings for me haven't changed, but the circumstances have. If she doesn't get the funding to avoid the eviction, I can see us having a hard time moving past that. I mean, can she really forgive me knowing I'm the one who played a prominent role in it?

Sighing, I try to focus on the present—on something I can actually control. So I help Paige zip up her jumper, watch as she slides into her heels. It's surprising to see her in a pair of heels;

she often swaps back and forth from her girlier side. Her room-mates are riding separately, since we can't all fit in Paige's tiny car, so they have already left. I'm stalling a bit with my makeup, taking extra-long to put on my mascara and blush, hoping the extra few minutes give me the courage I need. But I can only procrastinate so long, and I'm going to make us late. So I put my makeup away and wait for Paige to finish her look.

"Are you ready?" Paige looks at me as she slides on a pair of candy cane earrings.

"I think so." I nod. As ready as I'll ever be anyway.

TWENTY-TWO

Jax

My alarm wakes me with a start, and I feel like I've been sleeping for seven years. In reality, it's only been a few hours, and I still have time before everything starts. I jump right into the shower, not bothering to touch my phone. I take a relaxing shower and try not to think about how much is riding on tonight. But, of course, not thinking about it is sort of like thinking about it, too.

I put on my maroon button-down, my black pants with suspenders, and add a Santa hat for good measure. I try to soak up the Christmas spirit even though I am only hours from encountering Scrooge himself. I still don't know if El is even coming, but I do get notice that her father will be making it. It's not like we sent out invitations, but it's a small town and word gets around—especially that he is coming specifically to see the bookstore's downfall. I was even told he'll be bringing his father along, which is a rarity at this point. He isn't as healthy as my grandmother, so he is usually at the local nursing home.

When I show up to the library, the front doors have a sign instructing everyone to go around the side to the rec room, and there are balloons by the rec room doors. It has snowed, but not so much that no one can walk through it. And, thankfully, someone at the library has taken care of clearing all the accessible entrances of snow. The last thing we need is someone getting hurt on the way to help. I carry in the basket from the bookstore: a donation of several Christmas and holiday romance novels, bookmarks, stickers, and a gift card to the store. Which, of course, won't be of much help if the store closes.

"Hey! You look great." Parker smiles, taking the basket from me.

"You're here?" I ask, surprised.

"I came early to help out." Parker glances in her neighbor's direction, and I smile. She has it bad for this woman.

"Well, thank you. Everything looks great. I just need to make sure every basket has a silent auction form—"

"Already done, and every sheet has a pen—with ink that works—and there's a sign with instructions at every other basket as well so there's no confusion. I know how to follow a to-do list as well." Parker laughs.

"All right. I know I'm a pain; I just want this to go off well. It's sort of like my entire life is riding on this."

"I know. I do. But I'm your best friend; I wouldn't steer you in the wrong direction. Things are going to work out tonight." Parker smiles, and I try to relax. "Have you heard from El at all?"

"Not since her drunken phone call. Well, she's called once since then, but I was working and missed it," I lie. I saw the phone ring and choose not to pick up. I don't know what to say to her yet.

"And you didn't call her back?" Parker frowns.

"I just don't think it's a good idea to talk to her right now. I need to have all my focus and attention on this."

"Okay." Parker throws up her hands in surrender.

I glance at my watch and realize we only have thirty minutes until the event starts. Right now, only the staff is here, with the exception of Parker's neighbor's kids and extra librarians. I am nervous about how many people will actually show up tonight, but Parker says that, according to social media, we are on track for a good turnout. The table of baskets is full, the snack and dessert tables are being set up nicely, and the place looks extra festive. The DJ is already ready, and it looks like all we need are guests.

"Excuse me? Could we get some help?" someone by the door asks. I rush over and try to place them; they look so familiar, but I can't remember where I know them from.

"What can I help you with?" I smile.

"We're not sure where these baskets can go. We are told we can donate them, but no one explained where." She smiles.

"Baskets?" I look at her, confused, and then behind her to the blonde masc carrying two large baskets full of things.

"Can you remind me where you're from? I think we get all the donated baskets."

"Sorry, I thought you'd recognize me. I'm Bells, El's best friend. I run the orchard over in Sapphire Falls," the woman explains. My heart skips a beat at the mention of El. Is she coming too? I glance behind them, but I don't see her.

"Oh yes!" So that's where I know her from. "I didn't know you were coming, or bringing anything. I apologize."

"It's okay, El called last minute. One is full of apples, and the other is full of stuff from our bakery. Everything is fresh, and we think it can help," Bells explains.

"Of course, thank you so much." I usher them inside. "Head right over there, and the redhead, Parker, can help you with them," I instruct Bells's girlfriend.

"Is El here yet? I thought I'd be a little late, but there was surprisingly no traffic." Bells smiles, walking in and looking around.

"No, it hasn't started yet. Did she say she was coming?" I ask hesitantly.

"She better be! She called like an hour ago and asked if I could make it. I had to beg Tilly to drive us— I don't drive—but I'm sure you're used to that with El." She laughs, and I nod, so she goes on. "I tried to convince our friends to come, but they hate the winter. Makes sense with where they work; they're holed up inside once the cold weather starts."

"I can't relate; I love the winter," I admit.

"I'm happy in any weather. I'm just so glad I get to finally see this town. El always talks about it, but until you see it in person, it's hard to picture. I'm sorry for talking your ear off— you probably have a million things to do. I'll find you later whenever I see El, but please go take care of whatever you need to." She smiles.

"Thank you." I don't want to be rude, but I do want to make sure there is enough space for their baskets. Luckily, Parker looks like she is taking care of it, so I head to the front door and prop it open so any early people can come in.

"Jax!" I spin around when I hear my name, and a group of kids comes running toward me. They collide into me for a huge group hug, all of them talking at once.

"What are you guys doing here?" I ask, smiling. It is the snowball crew, all dressed up and supposedly here to support me.

"We told our parents to come!" one of them says.

"And we brought our allowance!" another adds.

"We want to help!" says another.

"You guys!" I smile. "You don't have to do that."

"We hear the bookstore might close. And we know how much that place means to you, so we want to help," they say.

"I appreciate that more than you know. But put your money away and promise me you'll just have some fun tonight." I look at each one of them.

"Okay, fine," they all grumble.

"Good. Now there's hot cocoa and cookies over there. Just remember to say thank you." I wink, and they all race over to the dessert tables.

It's one thing to see kids joining a snowball fight, but it's another when they show up for the community. You can say what you want about the youth of today, but these kids at least give me faith. Their parents are definitely raising them right. Not that I'd ever allow them to use their allowances on me, but it is the thought that counts.

As people start making their way in, I greet everyone, and I can't help but be on the lookout for El. Now that I know she is coming, it is the only thing on my mind. It is nice enough that she is coming, but to call her best friend in and have them bring baskets for donation too is extra kind. She must realize how important this is for me. It's so hard to think of her as one of the "Monroes" when she does stuff like this. It is like she is simultaneously two different people. Maybe that is what it is like for her: two different people fighting for the chance to do the right thing. Paige has overcome that, but she says it is harder for El. She is still holding out hope of making her parents proud, and I can't fault her for that.

I glance up, and that's when I see her, dressed in a beautiful red dress and the cutest pair of red heels. The dress shows off her body in the most modest way. I love that she doesn't shy away from her curves; she owns them. They are a part of her, and she knows they are beautiful. You can tell that by the way she walks and carries herself. Her red lipstick is still perfectly across her lips, and I am in awe of it. But I also want to see how messy it can get. I can't help it; she does something to me. When I look at her, I want to praise her but also want to see how bad she can be for me. El walks in with her sister, whom I don't give a second glance to. All my focus is on El, and nothing can tear me away from it.

"Hey, I'm so glad you can make it." I smile at her.

"You are?" She seems surprised, not that I can blame her. We didn't exactly have a good exchange the last time we spoke.

"I really am," I admit.

The people behind her try to get by, so she moves aside. "I should go in, but maybe we can talk later?" she asks.

"I'd like that." I nod.

El smiles, and I watch her enter the room. She casually walks through like she doesn't know the attention she commands. I am hopelessly a fool for her, and she doesn't even know it. Is this how it feels to love someone? All I want is for tonight to work out in every way possible. I need to save the bookstore and get my girl back. Hopefully, one won't cost me the other.

As if on cue, Mr. Monroe comes to the door with his wife on his arm. "Hello, Miss Evans." He smiles smugly.

"How are you, Mr. and Mrs. Monroe?" I force a smile. I don't want them to see how nervous I actually feel.

"Feeling very good tonight. I have a feeling I'll be booked with a brand-new property by the end of the night." He smirks.

"Have a great night, and don't forget to bid on some of the auction items," I say between clenched teeth.

He laughs and shakes his head, ushering his wife inside. I don't think I've ever actually heard her speak. She seems to be one of those wives who does everything her husband says to do, which includes being mute in public. I push out a deep breath and try to regain my peace.

"Why don't I take over greeting people, and you have a chance to talk to your girl?" Parker suggests.

"Thank you." I nod.

I look around the room and find El laughing with Bells, her girlfriend, and my grandma by the dessert table. She is eating a chocolate chip cookie and holding on to a cup of hot chocolate. I walk over and greet my grandma with a kiss on her cheek. I am glad to see her in such high spirits considering the day.

"I didn't know if I'd see you. I snuck in the back so I could avoid the crowd," my grandma explains.

"I thought maybe you fell asleep knitting again," I tease.

"Hey! A person my age is supposed to nap. Not someone so much younger than I am," she jokes back.

"Do you think we can go somewhere and talk?" I ask, looking at El.

"Sure." She smiles, puts down her drink, and we excuse ourselves.

We walk to the empty side of the room, out of earshot of anyone. I'm sure either way we'll be the talk of the town, but we don't need people listening in for details.

"I'm sorry about how I left—" I start.

"No, I'm sorry about my ex showing up," El cuts me off. "I didn't know she was coming, and it is a lot to put you through. She and I talked, and it's officially over. She's off the Ring camera and my lease, so she shouldn't be stopping by unannounced anymore."

"Well, that's good."

"Yes, because I'm hoping you'll be coming over more instead?" she says hopefully.

"Really?" I smile.

"Yes. I know there's a lot to consider, but I love you, Jax. It sounds insane because we've barely been together a month. But I feel like you wake me up. I've been complacent in my life, my job, my relationships, and you wake me up. I don't feel stuck or anything. I didn't even know that was something I needed until you walked into my life," she explains.

"You love me?" I repeat the words, making sure I heard her correctly.

"I do. And don't feel like you have to say it too because—" I cut her off with a kiss, our lips melting into each other's, and I can feel her body pressing into mine.

"I love you, too," I whisper against her lips.

She smiles, kissing me softly again. I take her hand in mine, holding it tightly the way I've been dying to all night.

"I know there's more to talk about but just know I'll do everything I can to get my father to drop this. And I'm willing to do everything I can to help you keep your store."

"We don't have to talk about this right now; I just want to be with you," I say desperately.

"I can't wait to be alone with you later," she whispers.

"Who says we have to wait until later?" I ask with a smirk.

"What…" She looks at me hesitantly, but I pull her hand tightly in mine.

"Do you trust me?"

"Of course," she says, not missing a beat.

"Then come with me." I lead her out the back entrance of the library. The winter air hits us as we head outside, and she looks at me skeptically as we walk down the street toward the bookstore.

Jax

"Lock the door," she whispers against my lips.

"What if we didn't?" I look at her with a wink.

"I—I don't know." She hesitates. "Fuck it." She pulls me in for another kiss.

"Mmm." I hum against her lips.

I unzip the back of her dress, the ruffled fabric sliding down my hands. Her sleeves start to shrug down her arms, and her dress puddles at her feet. She moves to pick it up, but I stop her, picking it up myself and carefully placing it on my desk. El is about to slip off her heels when I stop her.

"Keep them on," I whisper in her ear.

Loosening my collar, I tug off my tie and take the silk fabric in my fingers. I look to El for confirmation that this is what she wants, and she nods eagerly. I take the fabric and tie it around her head, covering her eyes.

"Can you see anything?" I whisper.

"Nope." She shakes her head.

"Good."

She's standing in just her panties, bra, and heels, and I have to remember to pace myself. She is just so fucking sexy. And I am the one in control right now. So I lead her to the chair behind my desk. She sits on the edge of the chair, both feet on the ground as she slides the chair across the floor. It is a quiet sound on the carpeted floors. I can't see her face, so I follow the sounds of her breathing and the moans she is holding back. Sliding my arm around her from behind, I reach for her chest first. She told me she wants this; it isn't like I am going to tell her no. I slide down a strap of her bra, and her breasts peek through. I grab one, nipples puckered, before I touch the other. Both of them over-flow in my hands. I will never be able to hold them both at once, but I have thought about it on more than one occasion—what it would feel like to put my face between them.

She moves her head back, but she can't see me, her eyes blocked with the fabric of my tie. Her brown hair is neatly tied in a tight ponytail that is falling into my lap. "Oh!" she whimpers.

"Mmm, that's a naughty girl. Didn't I tell you we have to be quiet in my store?" I smirk even though she can't see me. There is a thrill to this level of intimacy.

Even if you want to, there is no having sex with a stranger that is this intimate. Sure, you can explain your kinks, and they might try. But there is something different when you are with someone who knows you and your body so intimately. Knowing that she trusts me enough to be her eyes and hold her hands back is something I definitely have never felt in the past.

She hushes, and I pet the top of her head softly. "That's some-thing to put you back on the nice list."

El is quiet as she waits for me to touch her again. I unclasp her bra and toss it aside. Her breasts fall over her full stomach, and I peek over her shoulder to see her body from this angle. All curves, body rolls, and beauty. There is a beauty mark on the top of her breast that I will later get my tongue on. I slide my hands down her chest and tug roughly once more on her nipples.

"I want you to touch me," El whispers softly.

"Yes, baby." I slide my hand down her stomach and stop just above her pussy.

I can feel the heat radiating from between her thighs and kiss the side of her neck. El tilts her neck to the side, and I kiss it lightly as I move my fingers closer to her core. She is soaked, her panties wet through the center as I tease the top hem of them. I push my hand inside her panties and brush my fingers across her wet pussy. El gasps under me, and I nibble on her earlobe.

"Holy fuck," she whimpers quietly.

"Don't make too much noise, baby," I breathe into her ear.

She bites down on her bottom lip as I slip my fingers through her folds. She is so wet I want a taste. I take my fingers out, causing her to whimper in complaint, as I raise my hand to my mouth and suck her juices off my fingers.

"Mmm," I hum. She is so fucking sweet.

"D-did you just taste me?" she asks.

"Yes, and you taste so fucking good," I say in her ear, biting down and tugging on her earlobe.

"Oh, fuck." She moans.

I spin the chair around, and she is facing me. Leaning in for a kiss, I slide my tongue in her mouth, and she moans against me. Her hands reach for my body, and I push them back to her sides. She groans in frustration, and I kiss her neck softly before dropping to my knees.

"Lift," I command as I attempt to tug her panties off.

She lifts her ass, and I slide them down her deliciously thick thighs. I spread them, giving myself a direct path to her pussy, and I groan when I see her little landing strip, and I groan again as I taste her. El moans above me, and I slip her thigh over my shoulder, her red heels hanging over by my head. They are adorable, with white pom-poms on the top to look like Santa's hat, with a little golden bell in the middle. God, there is nothing fucking sexier than a woman in heels being eaten out, with her shoes hanging by my head.

"Oh yes!" El screams, and I have to stop licking her to scold her.

"I can't do this if you're not going to be quiet. Are you going to be a nice girl, or do I have to punish you, naughty girl?" I look up at El, and I know she is cursing me silently for stopping.

"I—I'll be quiet," she whimpers quietly.

"Good girl," I praise.

I go back to my spot between her thighs and lick her clit. El moans silently, and I continue dragging my tongue through her folds. Her head falls back in pleasure, and she is biting down so hard on her bottom lip I think it will be bleeding. Her breathing is heavy, most of it through her nose. My face is dripping with her juices, and I can't get enough.

"God, how the hell is it so much hotter not being able to see?" El whispers. But it comes out more as a whimper as I brush my teeth across her clit.

I don't speak, enjoying the moans and sounds coming out of her. El is the most relaxed I have ever seen her. She breathes life back into me as I feel her pussy grow wetter. I take two fingers, glide them through her, then push them inside her. She gasps, almost falling back in the chair. She bites her bottom lip again, and I smirk as I attach myself to her clit. I suck down on her sensitive bud, and she grips my hair. Tightly, she strings her fingers through my short curls. I know this means she is close. She doesn't want me to stop, and right now, there is nothing that can stop me from giving my girl pleasure.

"I want to see my naughty girl finish for me, but you have to be quiet," I whisper.

Looking up, El nods, and I swirl my tongue back around her clit. I suck, and her body comes to life for me. Her hands are in my hair, her thighs clutching my head like two soft pillows, and I watch her come undone. She puts her hand over her mouth, careful not to be too loud. The second her legs relax, she puts her legs down, the heels on the ground, and I look for a tissue to wipe my mouth. I am not going to embarrass her, but my girl is wet.

"Wow." El removes the tie from her head and smiles at me. She also unties her hair, letting her hair fall freely.

I lean in for a soft kiss, her lips tender from all the biting she has done to hold back her moans. Her hands find my chest, stopping to grab and squeeze my breasts lightly. My hands are on her ass, pulling her closer to me and steadying us from falling off her chair. She unbuckles my pants, sliding down the straps of my suspenders from each side. My shirt, with only one button left, is quickly undone, and that is shrugged off too.

"I can't wait to taste you," she mutters before dropping to her knees and sliding her body down so she is face-to-face with my pussy.

She pushes my underwear aside so she can dip her tongue into my folds. She moans, her brown hair cascading all around her as she tosses her head forward in pleasure. She takes long, languid licks up and down my folds, tight circles around my clit, and holds me by the waist to steady me. I feel like a live wire when she is going down on me.

"Oh!" I say a little too loudly, and she reaches her hand to cover my mouth.

"I need you to be quiet, or we'll have to lock that door," she says warningly, with a hint of teasing.

"Mmm." I agree. I will agree to anything right now if she just continues what she is doing.

"Fuck," she mumbles against me. I can feel her warm breath against my thighs as she positions my pussy right at her lips.

"I want you to wrap those thighs around my head and let yourself come for me," she commands.

"Mmm, okay," I say breathlessly.

"I want to see you shaking before I stop," she murmurs.

"I'm so close!" I call out, and she shushes me again, reminding me to be quiet.

"Baby, you have to be quiet, or someone might hear us."

"But you feel so fucking good," I groan. I didn't realize how hard it was going to be to be quiet.

"Do I need to take your underwear and stuff it in your

mouth?" She looks at me all sternly, like she's a teacher waiting to send me to detention.

I shake my head, and she smirks to herself. God, she drives me crazy. Her tongue connects with my pussy, and she slides in a finger too. I bite down hard on my bottom lip as I look down to see her staring back at me. I swear there is nothing sexier than watching a woman go down on you and seeing her look back at you. Maybe it is that there is nothing El can do that isn't sexy. Everything about her evokes this passionate response in me. She could be brushing her teeth, and just seeing those plump lips sends me into overdrive. I don't know how I spent so much of my life not knowing her.

El slides in a second finger as she sucks hard on my clit, and a moan escapes my lips. I can't stop it because my orgasm hits me like a freight train. My body convulses, my legs shake, and I'm gripping the sides of the chair so I don't fall off. El doesn't let up until I'm pushing her face away, unable to hold back anymore.

"Holy fucking shit, I love you," I moan.

"Is that all I have to do? Give you an orgasm and you love me?" she teases, standing up. She stretches out her knees and cracks her neck.

"You okay?"

"Of course; my knees are just not what they used to be," she laughs. "And the heels don't help."

"Oh, they help me for sure." I groan.

Taking El in, I want to commit this moment to memory: her standing naked in my office, except for her jewelry and a pair of red holiday heels; her breasts hanging against her stomach, pink with arousal; her stomach full of stretch marks and rolls that I know better than the back of my hands; her thighs dripping with her arousal. Her cheeks are a bright red, matching her red lipstick, and, surprisingly, her hair isn't out of place. Well, it started out in a ponytail, and somewhere along the way it ended up down around her shoulders.

"You are so beautiful," I murmur, pulling her closer to me.

"You are too," she whispers.

"I do love you, not just for the orgasms. I hope you know that." I tilt her face to look at mine.

"I know; I just like to tease you."

"Get dressed; we should probably be heading back. At some point my grandma or your sister will notice we're not there," I say.

"Or Parker." El laughs.

"Parker seems to be a little too preoccupied with the new librarian to notice anything else going on," I chuckle as I pick up my clothes.

"Ooo, the single mom? I never pictured that as Parker's type. I wonder if Paige can do a little matchmaking?" El plots.

"She might not need to; it turns out the librarian is Parker's new neighbor. They just moved in last week," I explain.

"Wow, well, go Parker." El smiles.

She turns around when her dress is on so I can zip it up. I do it slowly, then kiss the top of her neck when I'm done. I get a whiff of her perfume, relaxing me instantly. I have missed it this week without her. I don't want to admit it, but I don't know what I would do if El didn't come back. I thought I would be fine without her—I mean, we barely know each other. But the truth is, I have spent the last few weeks falling for her in ways I have never felt for anyone else. I never speak about my parents to anyone but my grandma, I have never brought anyone home before, and I definitely have never wanted to co-parent a cat with anyone else before.

I am not going to run back to New York and settle for less, but I also hope El will figure life out and come back to me. She makes me feel safe in ways I have never understood and awakens this passion in me. Maybe it is because we argue about so many things, or maybe it is just her personality, but I never want to argue with anyone else ever again. How could I, when I know what it's like to be with her?

"Come on," El says as she takes my hand.

"What about my tie?" I ask, looking at the tie on my desk.

"It's up to you, but in that unbuttoned shirt you look like a freaking model. I say skip it." She shrugs. My shirt is unbuttoned, showing off my tits. I normally wouldn't feel so comfortable wearing something like this, but with El I feel I can do anything.

TWENTY-FOUR

El

I'm pretty sure from the looks we get from Jax's grandma, Paige, Bells, and Parker, they all know what we were up to. It doesn't help that my hair is a mess and Jax is missing half her clothes. I don't shy away from her; people are going to talk about us no matter what. So I might as well get to hold my girl's hand in public. I told her I love her and then made love in her store. My panties are still soaked, and I am going to ravage her body later. But for now, we are back in public, and I need to focus on getting Jax through tonight.

"Nice to see you two getting along," Jax's grandma says with a wink, and everyone dies of laughter.

"Alright, thank you." Jax shoots her grandma a look while I giggle. "Do you want to dance?" Jax asks me.

"I'd love to." I smile.

Jax takes my hand, leading me to the dance floor, and my eyes are on her chest. She's wearing a simple black bra, and her tits barely fill it out, but God damn. I just want to lick up and down her chest right now.

"Hey, eyes up here," Jax teases.

"Sorry, my girlfriend looks so hot. I might have to be

punished later." I lean in, whispering into her ear. Jax shivers and grips my waist.

"Behave," she mouths quietly as we dance slowly.

Some Christmas song plays in the background while she holds me close. There are other couples dancing too, with the kids running around the dance floor. The place looks put together, and there are tons of people by the auction tables. My hope is that she pulls this off and I don't have to make some grand gesture. But my anxiety is getting the better of me, and I'm terrified what will happen if we can't pull this off.

After the second dance I excuse myself to look around. Jax gives me a look, like she knows what I'm up to, but I promise her I won't spend too much. I take my time looking at all the baskets, trying to find at least two I can place a high bid on. I finally land on the book one Jax has donated and the dessert one Bells has donated. They both have the most items, and it is actually stuff I'll use. I pick up the pen and bend over to write my name on the auction list when I feel someone come up behind me.

"You better put that pen down, Eliora," my father says in a warning tone.

"Seriously, Dad?" I grumble, turning to face him.

"Yes. I thought I made myself clear earlier. You're not to donate any of the Monroe money to this cause," he says with a hint of disgust.

"It's not Monroe money if I make it at my very lucrative job. You do realize I'm a successful lawyer, right?" I put my hands on my hips, waiting for him to back down.

"Even so, you will not make a disgrace of this family tonight by bidding in this auction. It's bad enough people are seeing you with an Evans." He shakes his head angrily.

"Is it really? Or are you making a bigger deal of this than it actually is?" I snap back.

"Excuse me?" my father says.

"El, dear. Let's just let this go for the night, please?" my mother jumps in. I didn't even noticed she was there, forever in the background unless she is playing peacekeeper.

"No. I'm tired of Dad being the boss of this family. He's literally tearing apart a family's livelihood and won't think twice about it. We don't need more money or more property, but they do need this bookstore. And I think it's insane Grandpa is holding onto this fifty-year grudge. It's time for us all to move on," I say angrily.

"I thought you were better than this. You sound just like your sister." He rolls his eyes.

"Why, thank you." I smile smugly before turning my back on him and writing my name and bid on the baskets. I only bid $1,000 each, figuring Jax can't be that angry at me. I only go over the last bids by $100 anyway.

"If everyone can finish placing their final bids, the auction is closing in ten minutes," Jax announces over the microphone. Parker and Paige have volunteered to count everything up so we can make an official announcement about whether we meet the goal or not.

"Do you think she's made it?" Bells whispers as I grab another cookie from the dessert table.

"I honestly don't know. I hope so." I take a deep breath. There isn't much I can do about it now.

"This town is awfully close to mine, if you ever think about moving back here," Bells says, wiggling her eyebrows.

"If you can't tell, Bells has been dying to get you closer. Apparently, I'm cool, but nothing compares to having her best friend close," Tilly jokes.

"Aww, you miss me," I tease.

"Oh, whatever." Bells rolls her eyes.

"I've been considering it. But I would definitely keep my place in the city, because I don't think I could live here full-time," I admit.

"Oh my God! Just having you close part-time again would be a dream come true!" Bells squeals.

I catch up with Bells and Tilly while Jax is talking to her grandma. Paige and Parker are in the library counting everything up, and I'm hoping things are going well. I'm half tempted to text them to fudge the numbers and have me cover the rest, but I don't. When they come out a little while later, I can tell by Paige's neutral face that things aren't good. Parker isn't letting on, so Jax has no idea; she takes the envelope from them with a smile and gets back on the stage. Jax has everyone's attention and is making a speech about being so thankful for everyone. But I can't hear it because all the blood is pounding in my ears. This is all my fault. I am about to lose the woman I love because I listened to my family instead of standing up for myself.

"Unfortunately, we did not make our goal, which means this is the last week of Reading Into It being open. I hope everyone will make a point to get down there before it's closed. Regardless of this outcome, it's meant so much to me to see the community coming together like this," Jax says. I can tell she is fighting back a bigger reaction. I just hope she'll still feel comfortable to let it go with me later.

Jax's grandma makes her way to the stage, and Jax hands her the microphone. She tries to leave, but her grandma holds her hand to keep her in place.

"So, my granddaughter has been busting her butt trying to save this place for me. And I'll forever be grateful for that. I didn't tell her this just in case we didn't need it, or in case it didn't work out. But I've just been informed that we got approval for Reading Into It to become a historical landmark in Evergreen Valley," Jax's grandma says proudly.

"All I need is a notary!" the woman next to her exclaims.

"Wait! I'm a notary!" my sister shouts, and my head whips in her direction.

"Over my dead body," my father shouts, but no one listens to him as Paige looks over the paperwork and happily takes the pen from the woman. Paige signs, and everyone is silent as we wait for someone to say something.

"Reading Into It is officially a historical landmark, and thus, being so, has more time to pay any outstanding bills and definitely cannot be sold or have the owners evicted," the woman announces, and the place turns into madness.

I watch as Jax picks up her grandma and hugs her tightly. Her grandma hits her in the arm until she puts her down. Then Jax races over to me, and the smile on her face is contagious. There are tears streaming down her cheeks as she pulls me in for a hug. I hold her close, and everything feels good and safe. It is like we've overcome everything we were so worried about. She holds my face in her hands and kisses me all over. I feel like I'm being licked by a puppy, but I don't even care. She's so happy, and I'm so relieved. Out of the corner of my eye, I see my father storming out with my mom. No one pays them any attention, but I know this is going to kill them.

"How did this all happen?" I ask Jax's grandma.

"I spoke to a lawyer when I get the eviction notice, and while there was nothing she can do about that, she mentioned it becoming a historical landmark. It needs to be fifty years old and have some sort of value or special characteristic to the community. When I mention it was one of the first-ever only romance bookstores, she started the paperwork," she explains.

"I can't believe you didn't tell me!" Jax shakes her head.

"I wasn't sure if it will work, or if the paperwork would come through in time," Jax's grandma says.

"And now, what? We have extra time to pay everything?" Jax asks.

"Yes, as long as we're making minimum payments, then we're good to go. And I have a feeling we'll be back on our feet sooner than later," she says proudly.

People come around to congratulate Jax's grandma, so Jax pulls me outside. Right under the cool winter night, she kisses me. With my body against the brick library building, she presses her body into mine, and I smile. I can't stop smiling, but she's smiling against my lips too. She kisses me with so much love and adoration I feel it through her lips. She doesn't have to say anything, and neither do I. Because both of us are relieved and in love.

"I'm so glad you walked into my bookstore with that bitchy look on your face and served me that eviction notice," Jax says, and I laugh.

"I did not have a bitchy look!" I exclaim.

"Oh, you totally did. You are hot, but a total bitch," she teases.

"I was trying to look tough!"

"Well, either way. I'm so glad we met and I melted that icy exterior of yours. Because I can't imagine my life without you now," Jax smiles.

"Oh yeah?"

"Mmm." She leans in to kiss me again, but this time I duck, grab a handful of snow, and chuck it right at her.

"That's payback!" I giggle.

"No, you didn't!" She chases after me, but I'm already grabbing more snow, so she grabs me by the waist and we're both falling into the snow.

Our clothes were already a mess, but now so is the rest of us. We're laughing like kids, and I feel the safest I've ever felt with someone else. I know I can laugh, and things are okay. I know tomorrow she's still going to love me, and that even if I can be a bitch sometimes, she's not going anywhere.

Epilogue I

JAX

1 year later…

"**I**f you keep cleaning it so much, it's going to rub the writing right off." El teases coming up behind me.

"I'm just making sure it's visible, even with the snow." I smile. El presses her red lips to mine and I relax a bit of my anxiety.

"It's not like it's a secret anymore. It's been a landmark with an official plaque for months now, and Andrea has all those posts about it. I'm sure people know." El reminds me.

"I know, you're right." I nod. I couldn't tell El the real reason behind my anxiety had nothing to do with the plaque. I'd been doing tasks like this to keep my mind busy and off what's actually bothering me.

"Are you headed home?" I ask, even though I already know the answer.

El opened her own law practice here in town, working part time to help people who are facing eviction from big companies. She does a lot of pro-bono work to counteract her father's work. While El still has her place in the city, when we're not staying there she rents it out like an AirBNB. It helps pay the rent and we like to use it too. El hasn't fully committed to small town living yet. She's got more than a few drawers at my place with Grandma, but she hasn't officially moved in. She and I call it home more often than not, but I know she might not ever fully give up her place in the city. I think she needs the security of knowing it's there. And as long as she wants me there with her, I don't really care where we live.

"Yeah, I was waiting for Paige to pick me up." El explains.

"Got it." I nod.

"Are you okay? You seem…jumpy?" El raises an eyebrow and studies me. I turn away quickly, hoping she can't read my face.

"I'm okay, just stressed about the holiday sales coming up." I lie.

"Oh okay." She doesn't seem convinced, but she doesn't put it any further either. "Well, are you coming home for dinner? Or are you still doing the inventory?"

I had been too nervous to spend any time with her this week and my ongoing lie was that I was handling the store's end of year inventory. I hated lying to her, but I knew if I was around her, I'd burst and tell her the truth. We weren't a couple who kept secrets from each other and I was not a good liar. Something I normally didn't care about.

"I have a bit more to do, but I'll be home for dinner." I smile.

"Okay, good." El smiles, leans in to kiss me and looks at me quizzically.

"I'm here!" Paige calls out from her car, pulling up in front of the bookstore.

"Oh my goodness where is he?!" El rushes to the backseat, ignoring Paige.

"I swear one of these days I just won't bring him." Paige rolls her eyes.

"I can't help it, I love my nephew." El scoops him out of his carseat and he's all smiles for her.

"Hi buddy, how are you?" I wave to him and he waves back.

"He loves auntie Jax almost as much as he loves auntie El, doesn't he?" El says in a baby voice. It's cute the way she gushes over him.

"Can you put him back in? I thought we were going?" Paige groans from inside the car.

"We are! I just needed a squish." El smiles. She gives me a quick kiss and I wave goodbye to both of them as she puts the baby back in the car.

Once they're all in the car and start driving away, I begin to relax. I needed time to set up everything and I only had an hour to get everything together. I grab my bag and head to the train station in town. Parker was already there setting up as much as she could.

"Thank you so much for setting up the lights! I was worried I wouldn't have enough time." I smile at my best friend.

"Don't even worry about it. The kids helped and I got to show off to Tess," Parker winks at her girlfriend who's helping her untangle the lights.

"I'm so nervous I almost told El what was going on, I was afraid she knows something's up." I breathe.

"She definitely knows, because you're the worse liar on the planet. But it's okay because in an hour or so she's going to be so happy she won't care." Parker assures me.

"You're right. I just hope she'll say yes."

"Are you kidding? Of course she's going to say yes. She's insanely in love with you." Parker chuckles.

"I hope so." I mumble to myself.

I knew El and I were ready for this. But I couldn't help the small voice in the back of my mind that had its doubts. It was like an annoying fear I couldn't seem to shake. Parker finishes hanging up the lights on the gazebo next to the train station as I set up the blanket. I also had a bottle of champagne, treats from the candy store and her favorite hot cocoa from Liz's Diner. I wanted this to be perfect, she deserved just as much.

"Is Paige bringing her?" Parker asks.

"Yeah, I have to call with a fake emergency. Paige will drive her and then I'll ask." I explain. We'd gone over the plan before, but I had changed my mind several times since deciding to propose. It was hard to pick the perfect everything to get this right.

"She's going to say yes, trust me this is so cute." Tess smiles coming up behind Parker.

"I hope so," I say.

El and I spent the better half of the last year saying hellos and goodbyes at this train station. We'd bring each other flowers, treats and hug until the very last second. I'd shed too many tears knowing I was going to miss her at this stop. So it seemed like the best place to do this. We would be moving on from our distance and finally settling down together. Even if we had two homes and lived between them, we'd finally be doing it together. And I was ready for any future that had El and I together permanently.

I glance at my watch and realize I need to call Paige. I dial her number and rattle off our fake emergency, giving her a chance to recite her lines and get over here. I knew I had about fifteen minutes and then El would be here. I pace inside the gazebo, the lights strung beautifully. Everything was in its place and everyone was hiding nearby. I hired a photographer from the city who would capture the moment and she was hidden nearby as well. I wanted to get the moment authentically, and I couldn't do that with her seeing the camera first. The snow in front of the gazebo is shoveled just enough to lead a short path so we can walk carefully.

"You can do this." I mumble to myself as Paige's car pulls up.

All the nerves I'm feeling disappear the second I see her.

El gets out of the car, looking around confused. She looks down the path toward me and I wave shyly. Her entire face lights up, cheeks raising into a huge smile as she sees me. She's wearing a different outfit than earlier, something I'm sure Paige tricked her into putting on. The green dress hugs her curves in all the right places, the sheer black tights teasing the delicious thighs I know she's hiding, and the heeled boots that click with each step against the pavement.

When she reaches me, I smile. "Hey."

"Hi," she giggles.

"Sorry about all the secrets, but I wanted this to be perfect." I explain.

"Is this why you've been so squirrelly all week?" She laughs again.

"Definitely." I laugh.

"You could've told me you wanted to bring me out here for a date. It's sweet, but why all the secrecy?" That's when I realize she thinks she knows, but she doesn't fully understand yet.

I drop to one knee in front of her and reach for her hand. She gasps, her eyes going wide and her right hand going to cover her mouth.

"Eliora Monroe, I can't put to words how happy the last year has made me. I never expected to meet you, let alone fall for you but I'm so glad that I did. You've taught me not to judge a book by its cover and appreciate all life has to offer. Will you do me the honor of marrying me?" I reach in my pocket for the engagement ring my grandma gave me and hold it up to her.

When I told my grandma I was asking Eliora to marry me, she only said two word; "about time!" Then she insisted on giving me her engagement ring to propose. She hadn't worn it in years but she always wanted to keep it in the family. I wasn't surprised since I knew how much she loved El. But it was a gesture that I'd think about forever. I knew El liked the finer things, and maybe she would want her own ring, but I had a good feeling about this.

"Yes!" El shouts and I put the ring on her finger. I'd had it sized against one of her other's so it fit perfectly.

I stand up and she pulls me in for a kiss. While her body presses into mine and I slip my tongue to hers, I hear an eruption of cheers behind us. Out from the shadows come Paige, Parker and Tess, Bells and Tilly, my grandma, and a horde of people from town. Everyone we'd become friends with over the last year and friends we've had before we met. Everyone we loved was by our sides ready to congratulate us.

"I can't believe you did all this." El's eyes tear and I squeeze her hand lightly.

"I told you she'd say yes." Parker winks before hugging me.

Everyone takes their time hugging and seeing the ring before we all head up the block for dinner at Liz's diner. I grabbed the bottle of champagne, toasting to our future while Max, our photographer got every intimate moment.

"I can't believe we're engaged. I thought you might be cheating on me with how crazy you've been acting." El jokes.

"I could never. I wouldn't want to, but I'm too bad of a liar to pull off an affair."

El and I laugh, her bright lips begging me to kiss them again.

"Is this your grandmother's ring?" She asks looking at the sparkly diamond.

"Yes, if it's not your style I can get you—"

She puts a hand on my lips, "Don't even finish that sentence. I love it. I recognize it from the photos of your grandparents wedding. It's so sweet she let you have it."

"She loves you like her own. She was quite insistent I give it to you." I laugh. El knows just how pushy my grandma can be.

"I'm glad she loves me as much as I love her." She smiles.

"I have another surprise for you," I whisper in her ear.

"What?" She looks at me quizzically.

"Tonight we're spending the night in a hotel, I already packed our bags. We have the whole weekend to ourselves." I tell her quietly. Her eyes light up and I can already imagine every dirty thought floating behind her eyes.

Epilogue II

EL

"Oh my gosh." Jax moans as I put my lips to her neck and nibble gently.

"You're so fucking beautiful," I whisper against her skin.

"I want you," Jax whimpers as I brush a hand across her stomach. I slide one of the straps of her bra off her shoulders and kiss along her bare skin. Something about her is addicting as hell.

"Mmm," she murmurs against me and I push her body back into the bed. I toss my dress off and throw it at the makeshift laundry pile across the room. I slide my tights on the floor and look directly at Jax as I unhook my bra and slip my panties down my thighs. She looks at me with mouthwatering eyes and a look of hunger I've never seen before.

"You're so fucking hot." She blushes, looking me over. I am pretty confident in my body, I mean I know I'm not everyone's body type but this was mine and I loved living in it.

Jax is laying on the bed with just her underwear on. "I want you to sit on my face, Naughty girl," she says with a smirk.

"Are you sure?" I whisper.

"Oh, I'm sure I want to taste you. I'm sure I want you to ride my face," she says, climbing onto the bed.

"Okay." I nod and lean in to kiss her.

Her lips are soft, her tongue slipping into my mouth at the last second, and I suck on it. Just enough to make her moan for me. I can feel my arousal slipping down my thighs and I am waiting for her to do something about that.

"Let me lay down, Naughty girl," She says, using the nickname again. She lies down on the bed and lays her head on the pillows. I look at her unsure, biting down on my bottom lip.

"Get on my face now," She commands.

Instead of speaking, I climb over her head, hovering my body on her face, and I can smell our arousals. Something about Jax had me like this all the time. She pulls my thighs into her face and starts sucking on my clit. I gasp out, tossing my head back as my thighs wrap around her head. She smiles underneath me, slurping up all of my juices with her tongue. She acts like she wants to enjoy every last drip of me, especially as I moan and groan with each touch. She edges her nose against my clit and I cry out.

"Oh fuck!" I call out and I know I'm closer than she should be.

Jax lets her tongue do most of the work, but she slips her hands on my stomach, up to my breasts and takes my nipples in between her fingertips. She tugs just enough to elicit some sounds from me.

"Oh Baby, I'm so fucking close," I call out and another swipe of her tongue through my slit and across my clit has me shaking over her.

"Fuck. Fuck. Fuck," I say, coming down from my orgasm and from off Jax's face. I pull her lips into mine.

"Mmm," She moans into my mouth and we both collapse into the sheets under us. "Don't go anywhere, I'm not done with you yet, naughty girl."

My eyes flicker open, wondering what she was up to. Jax

climbs off the hotel room bed and rifles in her bag, clearly looking for something. I almost think it's the strap, knowing she loves to fuck me with it, but instead she pulls out a candy cane. Did she need a mid sex snack? It wouldn't be the first time, but it seemed like an odd choice. I knew it was a few days before Christmas, but still.

"I want you to touch yourself with this, naughty girl." Jax says unwrapping it with her teeth carefully. The plastic falls to the floor and she climbs between my thighs.

Surely I haven't heard her right, "What?"

"I want you to slide this candy cane through your pussy and make yourself cum. If you can, and then I want to taste you until you scream." Jax says with a mischievous smirk.

It wasn't the first time we'd been adventurous in the bedroom. Hell I think we've done more positions than actually exist. But this was new territory. I take the candy cane from her, it's sticky and warm, some of the peppermint color rubbing off on her hands. I hold it up to her mouth, letting her lick the whole thing. Then I lean back in the pillows and spread my thighs apart.

Jax leans on the other side of the bed so she has a perfect view of the show. I slide it through my slick folds and shiver as I feel it against my pussy. It was a weird sensation. Sort of like when you eat a candy cane, but not? It was hard to describe because I'd never felt anything else like it. I twirl the end of it around my clit, watching as Jax's eyes widen in anticipation. Her breathing is tight and there's a consistent blush on her cheeks.

"You're such a naughty girl, you like it don't you?" She murmurs.

"I think you're the naughty one. You're the one watching and looking like you're going to explode." I tease.

"Mmm." She hums and presses her thighs together.

I slide the candy cane length through my pussy, letting it get completely immersed by me. I slide it inside myself cautiously. The last thing I wanted was for it to break apart inside me and ruin this moment. Jax's gaze locked in on it, watching as it slides in and out of me. The more the candy cane melts against my heat, the more I can feel it tingle. We'd once tried pop rocks down there—*which I highly don't recommend*—but this was different. It was almost like when you put on a Noxzema face mask, but instead of my face feeling tingly, it was my pussy.

"Fuck, I can't wait. I want to taste you." Jax pushes my hand out of the way, the candy cane falling onto the bed.

Jax licks slowly up and down my folds, taking in every drip of my wetness. "How do I taste?" I say breathlessly.

"Fuck, so damn good." She says in-between licks. "I didn't think you could taste any better."

I tangle my fingers in her hair and my new engagement ring shines in the hotel moonlight. I can't imagine a better way to break in our engagement than this. Jax singing between my thighs, the heat in my stomach building as another orgasm threatens to hit. All I want in this moment is to remember this forever. I watch Jax's back as she eats me out, all her back muscles on display. Her body is flexed, all her muscles working overtime as she brings me to the edge of pleasure. It's too much when she latches onto my clit that my head falls back and I cry out her name.

"Oh Jax!" I scream.

"God, I can't wait to do this for the rest of my life." She says before climbing up to kiss me. Her lips sloppily kissing mine, tasting like my pussy and peppermint.

"I love you Jax." I press my lips to hers.

"I love you more, El."

JAX

"You would seriously rather do this than engagement photos in the city?" I ask for the hundredth time. I knew El was pretty stubborn once she put her mind to things, but I wanted to be sure.

"We can take photos in the city anytime, but capturing our intimacy? To look back on when we're old and saggy? I think that's the best present ever." She smiles, her pink cheeks curling upward.

"Okay, I just wanted you to be sure." I kiss her cheek.

"Save that energy for when we're behind the camera." Max, our photographer, teases.

I met them when I was on a search for an engagement photographer. I fell in love with the pictures they've done on Instagram, but their most viral post is a boudoir shoot with a lesbian couple. It's two femmes who look equally sexy and in love. I loved the way Max captured them and hired her instantly for our engagement. Now that El had met her and did her own stalking, she begged for a holiday-themed lingerie shoot together. I was a little shy about it, but I knew I'd be comfortable once I was with El.

Max's studio was huge, with crazy high ceilings and lots of

natural light. Backdrops block some of the bigger windows off, probably to keep the sun from interfering in the photos. It's a little intimidating when you first walk in, but El grabs my hand and I begin to relax.

"Okay, so we have a makeshift changing room over here or a bathroom just down the hall where you both can change. We're only doing one outfit, so that helps with time. When you're done, just come back to me and I'll give you the rundown and we can start." Max smiles. They seem more relaxed today, being in their own space.

"Okay." El and I nod.

She leads me to the bathroom with her, and I change first. She already told me she wanted Max to capture my honest reaction on camera to her outfit. I can only imagine what she's wearing, so I get changed as soon as I can. El made me splurge, and I have a Calvin Klein matching black set. I'm wearing a pair of Christmas boxers over the underwear, but I'm mostly undressed. My biggest fear was my grandma finding these photos, but El reassured me we'd keep them at her place in the city locked away.

"Go, go, I need a minute to get ready." El shoves me out of the bathroom, and I walk back toward Max.

She's standing on a platform with a bed decorated for the shoot. It has dark green satin sheets and candy canes on the bed. There are canopy drapes over the bed with little snowflakes embedded in them.

"Is El okay?" Max asks, spotting me alone.

"Yeah, she actually has this idea of wanting me to be ready and waiting but you capturing my genuine reaction to whatever she's wearing." I explain.

"Oh, that's sick." Max nods. "So be careful of the step, but I think having you lounging across the bed would work best. Almost like you're waiting for her to get home."

"Okay." I climb up and slide across the slippery sheets. I wish I was wearing socks or something because I feel like I'm going to fall off the bed.

"Perfect, I'm going to set up the shot, so just ignore me. I want to find the right angle before I go grab El," Max explains.

"Okay," I nod.

Max clicks her oversized camera, and I try to relax, but I suddenly feel very aware of how naked I am. Like I'm covered as much as I would be at the beach, but it still feels off.

"Max? Are you ready?" El's voice carries from across the studio, and I feel instantly better.

This is how I knew she was the woman I had to spend the rest of my life with.

"Yeah! Come on out!" Max calls.

I don't bother turning my head because I know I'm not supposed to look. So I keep my eyes focused on Max and watch as I see red in the corner of my eye. I can hear the clicking of El's heels, making me wonder if her red ones with the Santa fur are making an appearance again. El was wearing a satin red robe that she's holding closed in the front. I can only see the tops of red lace stockings peeking out on her upper thighs. She's got a Santa hat in her hand and tosses it at me playfully.

"Put it on." She says. Truthfully, she could've handed me a bag of garbage, and I would've worn it.

I slide it on my head, tilting it to one side without letting my eyes leave hers. Max says something to her, but I don't hear it because I'm too focused on what she's got on under that robe. El unties it, shrugs it off her shoulders and my jaw drops. Underneath is a two-piece lingerie set I've never seen before. It's glittery and made of lace. There's the same material you'd find on a Santa hat all over the top and bottom of it. The bra barely contains her massive breasts, and the bottom is maybe a skirt, but not one you could wear legally into a restaurant and get served. It's connected to the thigh-high stockings she's wearing with two strips of red ribbon and metal clips. I wonder how much I could tear this outfit apart without her complaining.

"Holy crap, you look amazing. I'm a little pissed I have to share this with someone else." I joke.

El climbs onto the bed, and I'm only slightly aware of Max taking photos of us. Her breasts look like they're about to escape her bra with each movement toward me.

"You know I only have eyes for you babe," She climbs onto my lap, and I groan as I can feel her body finally touching mine.

I grab her ass, taking it with both my hands, and realize her panties are basically nonexistent. There's a bow above her crack, but it's really just a string. Fuck. I lean in and start kissing her neck, her breasts pressing against my chest as I lick the side of her neck.

"I've been a naughty girl; do you think I can still get on the nice list?" El whispers in my ear.

"Why don't you show me how nice you can be?" I say, looking up at her.

Her eyes catch mine, and I hold her face in my hands for just a minute. She was so beautiful; I wanted to remember this moment for myself. I lean in to kiss her, her hands roaming my body as I hold her steady on my lap. I relax under her touch, El grinding on my thighs. I could feel her wetness through her nonexistent panties. What I'd do to have her sit on my face right now. We'd talked about it beforehand and didn't want these photos to be erotic, just tastefully sexy. But I knew later on she'd be wearing my face like Santa's hat.

Acknowledgments

To Grandma, for inspiring Jax's Grandmother. For being just as supportive, if not more than her for all my writing dreams. She's just as stubborn, silly and loving as Jax's grandmother.

To Rieley, for creating this amazing book cover, I'm always in awe of your artwork. I knew you would knock this one out of the park!

To myself, for finishing this book through a breakup, my IUD literally rejecting my body and almost killing me, my son starting Kindergarten, and a summer of stress instead of sun. Sometimes I don't give myself enough credit for things but I'm really proud of myself and how this book came together.

To my readers, I thank all of you every single day. I couldn't do this without your constant and consistent support. It's been almost five years of me doing what I love professionally, and it still feels like a dream. From all of you who supported me since the first Christmas romance, to those starting out with me here, I'm forever grateful.

Also by Shannon O'Connor

SEASONS OF SEASIDE SERIES

(each book can be read as a standalone)

Only for the Summer

Only for Convenience

Only for the Holidays

Only to Save You

Seasons of Seaside: The Complete Collection

LIGHTHOUSE LOVERS

(each book can be read as a standalone)

Tour of Love

Hate to Love You

To Be Loved

Inn Love

Love, Unexpected

ETERNAL PORT VALLEY SERIES

Unexpected Departure

Unexpected Beginnings & Endings

Unexpected Days

Eternal Port Valley: The Complete Collection

STANDALONES

Electric Love

Butterflies in Paris

All's Fair in Love & Vegas

Fumbling into You

Doll Face

Poolside Love

BEHIND THE SCENES

(each book can be read as a standalone)

Eras of Us

Not My Fault

Bad at Love

EVERGREEN VALLEY

(each book can be read as a standalone)

Tangled Up In You

How the B*tch Stole Christmas

Santa, Baby

SAPPHIRE FALLS ORCHARD

(each book can be read as a standalone)

Sweater Weather

Accidentally Falling

THE HOLIDAYS WITH YOU

(each book can be read as a standalone)

I Saw Mommy Kissing the Nanny

Lucky to be Yours

The Only Reason

Ugly Sweater Christmas

POETRY

For Always

Holding on to Nothing

Say it Everyday

Midnights in a Mustang

About the Author

Shannon O'Connor is a twenty something, bisexual, self published author of several poetry books and counting. She released her debut contemporary romance novel, *Electric Love* in 2021. O'Connor is continuously working on new poetry projects, book reviews, and more, while also diving into motherhood. When she's not reading or writing she can be found watching Disney movies with her son where they reside in New York. She is currently a full time mom and full time author.
She sometimes writes as S O'Connor for MF romances and as Shannon Renee for Polyam romances.

Heat. Heart. & HEA's.

Check out more work & updates on:
Facebook Group: https://www.facebook.com/groups/shanssquad

Website: https://shanoconnor.com

facebook.com/AuthorShanOConnor

instagram.com/authorshannonoconnor

bookbub.com/authors/shannon-o-connor

pinterest.com/Shannonoconnor1498

threads.com/@authorshannonoconnor